White Satin

Lady

Imogen Pershouse

Dedication and disclaimer

White Satin Lady is a biological medical fiction book dedicated to raising social awareness of the devastating impacts of child abuse and serious food allergies. It is often underestimated the impacts these issues have on people's lives.

While this story is based on real life scenarios, any correlation to any real individuals or institutions is purely coincidental.

I am indebted to all those who helped me get this book published and my support people. Thanks especially to Percy, Viv, Jimo, Glyn, Kerry Collison, Marie Pietersz, Susan Pierotti and Luke Harris.

About the author

Imogen Pershouse is the pseudonym of a nurse who has worked forty-two years full-time in rural and tertiary hospitals in Queensland and New South Wales. She uses her extensive experience in general, midwifery and intensive care nursing in her writing.

Satin White Lady is her second book of medical biological fiction.

Other titles by Imogen Pershouse

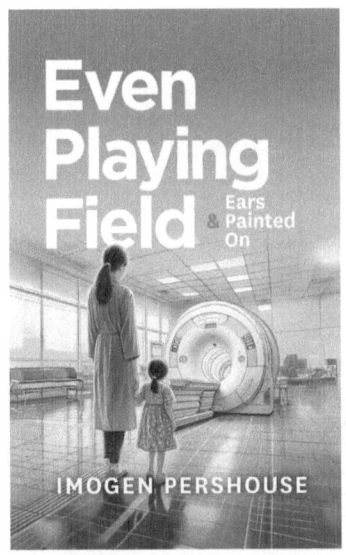 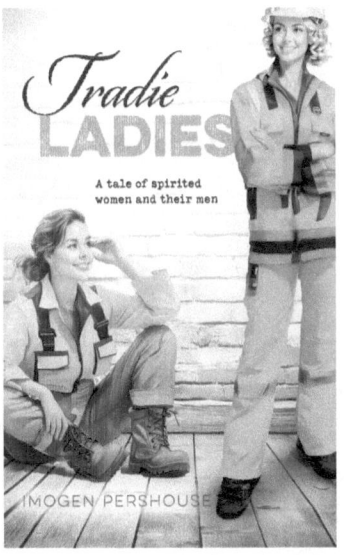

Even Playing Field,
Sid Harta,
ISBN: 978- 1-92295-8853

Tradie Ladies,
Sid Harta,
ISBN: 978-1-923439-02-3

Contents

Chapter 1	*The Barnett Family*	1
Chapter 2	*Chloe*	7
Chapter 3	*John and Bella Barnett*	10
Chapter 4	*Jake*	22
Chapter 5	*Vera*	26
Chapter 6	*Chloe*	29
Chapter 7	*Chloe*	33
Chapter 8	*Chloe*	47
Chapter 9	*Keith*	51
Chapter 10	*Sheila*	57
Chapter 11	*Chloe*	60
Chapter 12	*Georgie*	64
Chapter 13	*Irene and her children*	67
Chapter 14	*Keith's hospital visit*	72
Chapter 15	*Chloe*	85
Chapter 16	*Keith*	88
Chapter 17	*Chloe*	92

Chapter 18	*Chloe*	105
Chapter 19	*The Johnson family*	115
Chapter 20	*Johnson family conference*	138
Chapter 21	*The letter*	146
Chapter 22	*Slow progress*	149
Chapter 23	*The weekend at the Johnsons*	159
Chapter 24	*Sheila and Keith*	165
Chapter 25	*Keith and Chloe*	177
Chapter 26	*Keith and Chloe*	184
Chapter 27	*Chloe and Keith*	198
Chapter 28	*Irate Irene's reckoning*	204
Chapter 29	*Christmas*	213
Chapter 30	*Chloe*	225
Chapter 31	*Chloe and Keith*	228
Chapter 32	*Chloe and Willie*	241
Chapter 33	*Chloe*	247
Conclusion		253

Chapter 1

The Barnett Family

From the age of four, Chloe Barnett's life was a cycle of fear, grief and a struggle to survive.

Chloe's mother, Bella, had died at forty-two years of age, ten months after the birth of her little son, after breast cancer spread throughout her body. Relatively protected by the safe uterine environment, Chloe's little brother, Georgie, had lived, as his mother had refused the pregnancy termination that could have prolonged her life. However, Bella's siblings' reactions to her impending death inevitably skewed the family dynamics. While some family members were rapidly overwhelmed with escalating responsibilities, others milked the devastating crisis to their own advantage.

Due to her illness and a desire to leave gifts for her children, Bella was oblivious to the fact that her selfless decision had angered others. On hearing this news, Len's initial thought was that after Bella had died, as the oldest sibling with Power of Attorney of his parent's estate, he would use his status to divide their estate into two rather than three shares, eliminating the inheritance intended for Bella's children to increase his own wealth. Len's wife, Eve, held similar self-serving views. Eve applied for employment as a pay clerk out of town to remove herself from any obligation to assist in the care of Bella's dependent children. Since Len could get a transfer from his engineering firm, both were determined to distance themselves from unwanted burdens. With Len and Eve planning two future children of their own, both proactively exited this unfolding tragedy.

Even when they were small children, Len had always been self-orientated. Bella would pack a blanket and her teacup set to have picnics while her older brothers were fishing. Ross would help Bella by carrying one handle of the picnic hamper filled with drinks of cordial as well as small apple and mince pies, but never Len. Len would be carrying only his fishing gear. The thoughtful Bella always packed an extra apple pie to thank Ross for his assistance. When they were crossing the road at their school or church, it would always be Ross holding Bella's little hand to make sure she got to school safely. Ross always went the extra mile, while Len only participated in arrangements that benefited him.

Bella's other sister-in-law, Irene, a victim of a harsh childhood herself after her father had abandoned her pregnant mother, was angry. With six children of her own, Irene already had her workloads maxed, before her husband Ross asked her to assume a five-day week responsibility for Bella's children. After Ross went to work, the fuming Irene was left raising ten children. Exhausted from caring for their own six children, the last thing Irene needed was another four children under eight years old invading her home. Bella's family had supported Ross's notion for him and Irene to raise Vera, Jake, Chloe and George without offering any support themselves, for the care of ten children under eighteen years. Bella's elderly parents, Stan and Mabel, who were in their eighties, had volunteered to care for their dying daughter. This allowed Bella's husband, John, to earn his minimum wage as a railway fettler.

There were no social security benefit schemes available in the 1960s to raise his children himself, as he would have preferred. Therefore, John, an uneducated man, paid Irene and Ross half of his wage for the care of his four children from Monday to Friday. This arrangement enabled Ross and Irene to purchase a larger house, capable of accommodating the ten children. John keenly resumed the custody of his four children every Friday afternoon as soon as he finished work, returning them Sunday evenings. This arrangement allowed Ross and Irene every weekend to dedicate time to their own children.

While Ross as a full-time boilermaker was happy to comply with Bella's wishes for her children not to be raised separately in different households, the cantankerous Irene was livid. The last thing she needed was another four intruders. From Irene's perspective, Bella had made a selfish choice to save her unborn child, particularly since it had meant unloading onto her four spoilt children. Possessing absolutely no grace about this situation, Irene's moans about all the cleaning, washing, ironing and cooking workload fell on deaf ears. With Len and Eve conspicuous by their absence, and their grandparents looking after their dying daughter, discipline was left up to Irene.

Although the sanctimonious Irene told her neighbours, church goers and anyone who would listen that she would control these ungrateful children by any means possible, all underestimated the level of abuse being inflicted. Irene displayed no hesitation in pulling any of the children's pants down in the street to beat them black and blue, since her violence was never challenged. At any slight, Irene resentfully sent Bella's children outside to fill buckets of weeds as punishment, to remove them from her home.

When the stress of a hostile environment caused Vera, Jake, Chloe or George to chew their nails, Irene would put their tiny fingers in chicken manure then forcefully return the soiled fingers into their mouths. All four Barnett children were terrified of Irene's beatings with the wide strap and stinging wooden spoon. If a milk bottle was found knocked over in the fridge, all the 'aliens' would get belted every hour until one confessed. Often as the oldest, Vera, to her own detriment, would confess to the crime most likely accidentally perpetrated by Irene's own children, to safeguard her younger siblings.

Soon, the aggressive Irene was dealt another devastating blow. Her youngest son, Robert, who had been experiencing breath-holding episodes since birth, was diagnosed with four abnormalities in his heart. With this congenital condition, called a Tetralogy of Fallot, not amenable to treatment in the 1960s, Irene worried excessively each time Robert assumed crouching positions to relieve his breathlessness. As Robert's lips and fingernails became more bluish from oxygen lack, unable to walk much, he spent his days playing stationary games like marbles.

However, at three years old, the amiable Robert's mental agility was often underestimated. Robert would play practical jokes on his unsuspecting siblings and cousins. When Chloe left their marbles game, distractedly watching a bird hovering near the flower garden, Robert peed into the water pistol Chloe often drank from.

When Chloe spat out the oily tasting pee, other children entertained by Robert's prank roared with laughter. After Robert was sent to bed without his evening meal as punishment, overwrought from crying, his fragile heart decompensated. Robert died silently alone and unobserved.

Stricken with grief and the guilt attributing to Robert's demise, Irene began bonding with the now one-year-old Georgie. Since Georgie had been only ten months old when Bella died, he readily returned the affection. Thus, Georgie was afforded more protection in this dysfunctional household, as Irene filled the void from Robert's death with nurturing him. Unlike Vera, Jake and Chloe, Georgie got no plates smashed over his head when crockery sets were dropped or chipped accidentally. He received fewer beatings when wood accidentally slid out of the wooden stove door, melting the new kitchen lino. Consequently, the healthy Georgie was saved by instinctively returning the affection he received from Irene, the only mother he had even known.

Not only did these children not really bond together as Bella had hoped, the sheer brutality inflicted by Irene on the rest of the Barnett children left lifelong physical, social and psychological scars. Even minor infringements like walking on the carpeted stairs to their bedrooms too often saw the children disciplined with filling buckets of weeds or belted. Living under such oppressive conditions, the Barnett children looked forward to going to school and eagerly waited for weekend visits with their father.

Chapter 2

Chloe

After being repeatedly subjected to extreme brutality and denigration, Chloe ran away so many times John soon realised it was not worthwhile returning her to Irene's. Chloe's first escape occurred after Irene had roughly ripped stitches out of her foot, as retaliation for the eight-year-old not reminding her of an appointment for suture removal. Chloe had sustained the wound after standing on broken glass buried in mud when fishing with her father and siblings. However, after the hospital had diplomatically notified Irene of the missed appointment, Irene had viciously lashed out at the child. Embarrassed at forgetting the appointment, Chloe was paralysed with fear when the untrained Irene roughly removed the stitches herself. Over the years, Chloe had been victimised by Irene relentlessly, as her dark hair, oval face and chocolate eyes mirrored her mother's image. In Ross's absence, Chloe, Jake and Vera were constantly told during beatings that their presence in Irene's house was the result of their mother's foolish choice not to terminate her pregnancy.

No amount of beltings or empty promises could encourage the strong-willed Chloe to stay in the vicious household ruled by Irene. Chloe absconded first, soon followed by Jake, Vera and finally Georgie. While all the children were treated well during their father's weekend custody, where they were allowed sweets and played games, reporting Irene's violence was futile.

Although Irene had blatantly promised John that there would be no reprisals for his children's flight to safety, her pledges only lasted until he left. Any child who had absconded would then be slapped across their face repetitively, until their cheeks stung and they begged for mercy. Ross's attempt to lock Chloe in the bedroom she shared with the other girls only delayed the inevitable.

The long-term impact of Irene's brutality was that all the Barnett children had difficulties trusting and bonding in peer or partner relationships. From an early age, all the Barnett children had seen and survived humanity at its worst. All knew better than to accept people's advice or promises at face value. As the children got older, they all began regularly running away from Irene's cruelty to the safety of their father's house. Each time John returned Chloe to Irene's house, her face was brutally slapped. Chloe, therefore, ran away again in terror, returning faster than John could to his own house. Her profound fear of Irene was undoubted, as Chloe trembled and shuddered uncontrollably each time she entered her gate.

Finally, John asked for Chloe's clothes to return home with. From Irene's self-righteous diatribe, John recognised that it was Chloe's appearance of being Bella's clone that was triggering abuse rather than bad behaviours. Having escaped Irene's tyranny, Chloe remained living in the house with her father. From twelve years of age, Chloe became fiercely resilient and independent. She was capable of riding to school alone, getting groceries and doing household chores. Since John's employment hours of 7 am to 4 pm were relatively compatible with school timeframes, with the assistance of friendly neighbours, the arrangement worked well.

Having secured a safe environment, Chloe began to excel in scholastic achievements, winning senior prizes for science as well as statewide awards for assignments. To feed her growing passion and fascination for science, Chloe hoped to explore a career as a laboratory scientist. Chloe was attracted to both the idea of working in a pathology department analysing body fluids and disease processes as much as a career option that allowed social isolation. Focusing on study and science simultaneously would limit her interaction with the human race she had no faith in. Chloe was too traumatised by her early negative experience with cruelty to believe human nature capable of change.

Chapter 3

John and Bella Barnett

John Barnett at fifty years old was 180 cm tall. He had been thirty-six years old when he had first met the gorgeous, petite Bella at the Gayndah railway station travelling home to visit her parents in Gympie. John first spotted the raven-haired beauty battling to lift a large suitcase from the platform into the railway carriage. Her shiny, wavy hair was blowing up in the gale, obscuring her vision. Just as John strode towards her, Bella landed the heavy baggage back onto the platform, unable to lift the heavy item to the required height.

'Thank you so much, sir,' the respectful young lady had gratefully replied.

'You're welcome, ma'am.'

The charming John stood smiling, waiting to shut the carriage door as Bella ascended the three steps onto the train due to depart. Another gust caused her cobalt blue chiffon dress to fly upwards. John averted his gaze but not before seeing the flash of her trim legs unexpectedly revealed. Their mutual attraction had been immediate.

John and Bella became engaged three months later and married after six months. John's tall height, toned build, fair complexion, gold auburn hair and vivid blue eyes fascinated and captivated the shy Scottish-born Bella.

In terms of their backgrounds and skills, Bella and John were polar opposites. While John's skills were more externally focused on gardening, farming and carpentry; Bella was more creatively and intellectually inclined. Bella played the bagpipes she had learned from her maternal grandfather, enjoyed photography and loved reading. She also loved cooking. She could make pasta in the traditional way, taught to her by her paternal Italian grandmother. Bella knitted, crocheted and learned most crafts. Whether it was teaching Sunday school children or John to read and write, Bella displayed infinite patience.

John's eyes lit up and his face beamed with his charismatic smile each time they met. Bella would warmly smile back and wave her tiny hands, as he approached to greet her when they saw each other in shops and at the local school fundraisers. Right from the get-go, Bella and John had got along fabulously. As they began formally dating in Gayndah, Bella and John soon discovered they had many friends in common, both at the Sunday school where Bella taught the local children Bible classes and at the dances. Every Saturday night, they had loads of fun with their friends, learning the latest dance crazes or all viewing the latest cinema movies.

However, John had always found any interaction that included Bella's family challenging. Bella's siblings and parents seemed obsessively preoccupied with social image and expectations rather than simply enjoying life. Bella and John had not even been able to marry without their oppressive power games. While Bella wanted to marry among their friends in the small Gayndah church, her parents, supported by her brothers, had demanded the full Methodist ceremony in Gympie, despite John's Salvation Army upbringing. In trying to please others, Bella's happy day was ruined.

Pleasing Bella's family had ridiculously inflated their wedding costs, absorbing most of the funds that John and Bella had frugally set aside for their honeymoon trip to Sydney. Although they had already paid their travel and accommodation costs, they were left with barely enough for food. However, despite fewer funds for some of the day tours planned, they still enjoyed wandering around the big city shopping centres and tourist attractions. Bella had brought her camera to catch the special moments they had shared at the Harbour Bridge, Opera House, Taronga Park Zoo, The Rocks, Manly and Circular Quay.

Too much of John's income had gone towards church fees and an elaborate ceremony, expenses both had hoped to avoid. Stan and Mabel had ardently insisted that the wedding of their only daughter needed to be a social occasion, orchestrated to boost the family's status in the Gympie community. Their views had contrasted vastly with the intimate church service with friends Bella had wished for. However, Bella and John had not realised then that the ambush of their wedding would be just the beginning of their treacherous interactions with her inflexible family. As the only daughter, John had witnessed during their family dynamics how Bella's clever ideas were typically overridden by her two brothers' opinions.

Over the years, with the birth of each healthy child, Bella and John's happiness grew. They blissfully loved each other and enjoyed sharing their family moments together. Both actively participated in caring for their children, enjoying many picnics and visits to the local parks and zoo.

When the doctor had called John and Bella in for test results during Bella's fourth pregnancy, they had both been naïvely keen to learn the gender of their unborn child. Neither had imagined that the lump in Bella's breast would be a malignant tumour invading her body. John had mistaken the doctor's serious expression. He had wrongly assumed the concerned obstetrician to be just the stern, educated type.

'Bella and John,' Dr Finnegan began hesitantly, 'I have some alarming news …'

Taken aback, John had looked at Bella. This was not at all what he was expecting to hear. Two severe faces gazed back at him.

'Unfortunately, your left breast test has revealed you have a cancer, Bella.'

John's whole body ran cold with fear. Just when he had finally settled down with a mortgage and a lovely home to bring up their beautiful children, life had thrown the ultimate curve ball.

'But ya can sort it, right?' John asked, keen for solutions.

'Well, we need to discuss the choices you and Bella wish to make first,' clarified the doctor. 'Specifically, I need to ask whether Bella wishes to terminate this pregnancy or not. I am very concerned that you will need aggressive treatment to survive this, Bella. There is already a spot on your lung.'

'Cancer, you mean ... has spread from my breast to one of my lungs?' questioned the distraught Bella. One hand gripped John's tightly while the other subconsciously migrated to her left breast.

'Yes. If we terminate the pregnancy, we might be able to extend your life by shutting down potential hormonal spread. That could give you another ... maybe up to two years, to bring up your young family,' the doctor factually responded.

'If I didn't terminate the pregnancy ... what would my baby's chances be?' inquired the acutely distressed Bella, not keen to be killing her unborn child.

'If you survive the pregnancy, your baby is at a lower risk, due to the protection afforded naturally by the intrauterine environment. Your baby would most likely be unharmed. Most cancers, generally speaking, do not cross the placental barrier. The incidence of that happening is rare.'

'I cannot kill my baby,' cried the devastated Bella, pleading at John tearfully before looking again at the troubled doctor. 'Please don't ask me to do that ... I could never kill a sacred child that God has gifted me!'

'What can we do, doctor?' John asked, putting his arm supportively around his now sobbing wife.

'It's quite a predicament really. Any drugs that we give Bella to treat the cancer may adversely affect her unborn child. Drugs that fight cancer stop cell division. So, we cannot treat Bella aggressively while she is pregnant without potential harm to the baby. The baby's cells need to be able to replicate for growth. Many anti-cancer drugs stop cell replication.'

Profound silence ensued.

'So, in three months' time when I have my baby, I might be able to get treatment?' Bella asked optimistically.

'Three months of pregnancy hormones disseminating cancer can do a lot of harm, Bella. I think it best if you both go home and think carefully about this decision. It is not one that should be made hastily or lightly.'

'But, doctor, you say the cancer is already spread to my lungs, right? So, we know that I am going to die sooner rather than later,' suggested Bella. Bella's devout religious faith was vital in helping her face her own mortality. 'How long do you think I could live after the baby is born, if I go to full term?'

'Three months, maybe a year. However, performing surgery to remove the primary breast lump where the ductal invasive carcinoma is, while you are pregnant, is less likely to be effective. The secondary lung tumour needs therapeutic radiation.'

Dr Finnegan paused before saying, 'I have discussed your case with other specialists, and they have suggested that hormonal chemotherapy or therapeutic radiation would pose a risk to your unborn child, while you are still pregnant. Unfortunately, there has not been a lot of research on cancers during pregnancy. Due to the young age of child-bearing women, this situation is uncommon. The consultants I spoke to advised that a caesarian section at eight months could give you both the best chance of survival. Most of the scientific data suggests that in the uterine environment, there is a lower risk to the infant. However, that is not absolute. In a Japanese case, cancer crossed the placental barrier, but this is extremely rare. I would therefore suggest we talk again tomorrow, after you have had time to think about this decision. If you still want to proceed then, we will organise the caesarian section in your eighth month of pregnancy.'

John and Bella returned the next day, sadly accepting this dismal plan, both despairing of the outcome.

Bella had four wishes that John lovingly made his priority. Firstly, Bella wanted to organise gifts for Vera, Jake and Chloe and their unborn child. Secondly, Bella asked John to transfer back to Gympie where she had ambitiously hoped there would be more support for John and the children. Thirdly, instead of Christmas gifts, Bella asked her family to pay for final family photos of her with Vera, Jake, Chloe, Georgie and John, with extra copies of the originals purchased and stored for their children. Finally, Bella wanted her children to be raised together, after John's family members had offered to raise only one of the four children each. It was the final request that catapulted John's anxiety to toxic levels.

Still reeling from Bella's diagnosis and her poor prognosis,

John felt helpless. The best he felt he could do was to respect his wife's wishes, while praying for courage to endure the imminent crisis. John believed that if Bella had the dignity to die with absolute faith in her Christian beliefs, then he would cope somehow also.

However, John struggled with the unrestrained hostility he received from Bella's parents and brothers on their arrival in Gympie. As a rural farmer living on remote properties during the war, John had received very little formal education. Now, John got along, with Bella's help, by just being able to sign his name. Being uneducated, with extremely limited literacy skills, John was initially grateful when his foreman arranged the transfer for him to return to Gympie. They had placed their Gayndah home on the market and began organising another mortgage on a suitable low set house in Gympie. In this overwhelming upheaval, nothing could have prepared John for the hostility that met them after they had relocated.

With Bella's health deteriorating, John was dependent on her opinionated brothers, Ross and Len, to help him by reading the mortgage documents. All the members of Bella's family were keen on spouting their judgmental opinions, about his supporting Bella's decision to spare their 'unknown child'. John was berated about this choice 'compromising Bella's wellbeing and affecting the life opportunities of their other children'. John had heard their ill-informed opinions often enough.

Since Bella's family was not present when the doctors had discussed her options, their ignorant attitudes were not welcome. John loved Bella and all their children immensely.

He was in such a quandary after the news that he could never have made any decision. All John knew was that he needed a miracle. So, John prayed intensely, willing them all to survive. John was so overwhelmed and grief-stricken by the unexpected news that the sad decision was made by Bella and the doctor, based on science and statistics. Bella's unwavering Christian beliefs and blind love for her family and extended family had made her decision easier.

Tragically, in the extreme circumstances, John was stunned to discover that he had started grieving for Bella, even while she was still alive. This grief was compounded after Bella had to leave their new Gympie home, to be cared for by her parents. Their spiralling debts had rendered John powerless. He needed to continue working to pay off the enormous debts that were mounting. John had never felt so utterly defenceless. He had always preferred living in the rural town of Gayndah, where the cost of living was cheaper, than closer to Bella's domineering family. Bella's family constantly overrode his wishes as readily as they had disregarded Bella's.

However, with Bella having given birth to their three children and being pregnant again with a terminal illness, relocating and complying with her few wishes seemed the least he could do. Fortunately, Bella was so sick that she was oblivious to the undertones in her family's judgmental communications.

After Ross had suggested that he would require half John's wage to raise his children five days a week, John was left with very little income after the transport couriers, mortgage payments and Bella's funeral. John also loathed having Irene care for his children, especially when she referred to them in demeaning tones as 'spoilt and undisciplined'. However, with his wife sacrificing her life for their unborn child, John could only do his best. Bella naively had a more upbeat opinion of her siblings and parents than John ever did. Having grown up with affectionate, doting parents who were now deceased, John considered Bella's family emotionally cold, disapproving and unforgiving.

Unfortunately, all parties had underestimated the high expectations thrust upon Ross and Irene, who were left managing ten children under eighteen years of age. While Irene had wanted a greater income to supplement Ross's meagre wage as a boilermaker, she had no interest in bringing up Bella's children. In Irene's inflexible mind, those children were Bella's responsibility. Bella should have made a better choice that did not impact on her quality of life.

When John witnessed how Bella's family lacked compassion in their treatment of his dying wife, he cried nightly fearing for the safety of his vulnerable children. Given the choice, John would not give that religious zealot Irene the time of day, let alone a minute of custody of his adorable sons and daughters. Even Irene's scowls filled him with dread. John did not believe he could trust a single word she uttered. Irene was as devious as she was cruel. Right from the beginning, his children were fearful, demonstrating guarded and vigilant behaviours. While Bella had raised their children with nurturing and love, Irene was beyond harsh.

The first sign of trouble for John was the reactions of his four-year-old Chloe. She liked riding on his steel cap boots, grasping his trouser leg as he walked. One day when doing this, Chloe suddenly flinched visibly as he went to get his wallet out of his back pocket to pay for groceries. In defensively protecting her face, Chloe fell over when she let go of her hold, as John had unwittingly kept moving. Another time, Vera, Jake and Chloe screamed and ran when John pulled the belt out of his trousers on the bed to thread it into the set he was wearing. On another occasion, while running the bathwater, John was alarmed to see that Vera had a reddened straight line across her back from a belt. When he returned his children on the Sunday evening, John sincerely hoped he had addressed Irene's behaviour by asking her subtly to be kind to his children.

John's feeling of helplessness grew as his children got older. Individually, they all began running away to his home to escape Irene's abuse. It was beyond frustrating having to return them to someone John absolutely hated. However, he was virtually destitute. Always struggling financially, John felt he had no choice other than to return his frightened children, as he needed to keep his full-time fettler position in the railway. In the 1960s, there were no social benefits for widowers to care for their children themselves. You had two choices: you were either employed or homeless.

John's conscience was constantly tormented and unsettled. His children's behaviour and the belt marks had confirmed that he had delivered their innocent babies into the bowels of hell, with the devil, Irene, as their carer. John's only choice was to go without. In doing so, he was able to save meagre amounts to escape with his children out of town to his own family on school holidays, using the free railway passes that were an employment benefit. Unable to drive, John rode a pushbike everywhere. Each week, he bought either mince or sausages and vegetables, depending on what was cheapest. John cooked only two rissoles or sausages a day to ensure his rations lasted until the next payday. Any savings that did not go to their family holidays out of town went to weekend treats to buy grapes, strawberries, bananas or mandarins for his children. John barely scraped enough together to pay the electricity and gas bills.

For Irene, fear, guilt and pain motivated children, not love. Children did not get choices; they did as they were told, or they got punished. There was no need to 'manage grieving children's behaviours'. Discipline was all they needed, and she was extremely motivated to provide it. Religion to Irene was a tactic manipulated to obtain social acceptance. Faith was a luxury she had never afforded. Historically, Irene had been brought up in a Victorian household where discipline was strict. Although John prayed desperately every night that Irene would show his children mercy, the rod (or belt) was not spared. It was a case of God help each child!

Chapter 4

Jake

With Georgie seeming to be at a lower risk of assaults and Chloe now living at our father's house, I left school at fifteen years to accept employment in the rural industry. When I was offered a posting to New South Wales, I gladly accepted. The further I was away from the toxic Irene and her family the better! Through my gentle 'peace at any price' nature, I avoided conflicts. I preferred to show kindness to others, volunteering with several charities like the Apex Club on my days off. My one weakness was an inability to develop any tolerance for people who were irrational or emotionally hard work.

Over ten years of Irene's bible bashing and 'holier than thou' stance had left me unable to enter, let alone, marry in a church. I had no regard for hypocrites who could preach 'God is love', then witness children being physically and psychologically abused without intervening. While churchgoers watched Irene with disdain as she seethed and raged, justifying and boasting of her violent punishments, not one of them challenged her conduct. Nothing can justify plates being wilfully smashed on a child's head to pacify a bad mood – not then, not ever. I had suffered a splitting headache and nausea for days afterwards and vomited when she forced me eat.

In contrast to my siblings, my survival strategy at Irene's was hiding under the radar. Although this self-preservation strategy reduced my beatings, my self-esteem plummeted. Apologising profusely or pleading for mercy was pointless. Irene relished any opportunity to weaponise any object at hand. Tragically, we counted our blessings to get hit with the strap of the belt rather than the buckle which hurt and bruised more.

After leaving Irene's, my life's ambition was to never see her or her family *ever* again. I was determined to steer clear of both Irene's pathology and the Christian inertia that had plagued our childhood. Desperately hoping to mobilise anyone, someone, to intervene, we had once told the neighbour's children how Irene had intentionally dumped their cat in a park on the other side of town. Irene had vehemently blamed the innocent animal for the stench in her car, accusing it of urinating on the tyres. However, when the stench remained, Irene found the offensive odour was emanating from raw mince that had fallen under the front seats of her vehicle, after she had loaded groceries on the back seat.

As an adult, I controlled my choices. Prior to my marriage to Wanda and the birth of our lovely daughters, Sally and Sarah, one thing was non-negotiable: I would never enter a church again, dead or alive. All my family and siblings understood that regardless of the circumstances. However, I consented to Wanda's request to have our daughters raised in a Lutheran school, which was fine. My issues with religion were not so much against the institution itself but with the worshippers' interpreting the gospel for their own convenience and benefit.

In marriage partners, I chose someone who did not deliver the sarcasm and denigration I had endured for my whole childhood. I wanted my family to develop relationships with therapeutic communication, where all family members felt valued and respected. I had retained a few fond memories of my loving mother doting on us and playing in the park. I actively sought that childhood concept of normal.

The life I lived was very compartmentalised. In my employment life, I existed by keeping my opinions to myself. My 'peace at any price' mentality also persisted during my charity work with other volunteers. Mostly, I led a quiet life with the goal of avoiding conflicts.

As an adult, when I observed Irate Irene at a shopping centre loudly denigrating my siblings as 'ungrateful children', I recognised how absurd she actually was. Desperately seeking unwarranted attention, Irene was praising her own children's accomplishments loudly. Irene was oblivious to the fact that my siblings were just as qualified as our cousins, if not more so. It was interesting to observe how much she lacked insight or awareness. Irene was totally oblivious to how many individuals consciously detoured to avoid any interaction with her. Others seeing Irene too late pretended to dig frantically into their handbags or looked away to avoid engaging in conversations with her. From Irene's bewildering perspective, she considered she was owed a debt of gratitude for never having mastered sophisticated elegance, proper decorum or empathy.

It was an interesting spectacle to watch from a distance.

Chapter 5

Vera

I abruptly left Irene's at fifteen years old by accepting a butcher shop assistant vacancy to escape her daily maltreatment. For Chloe and me, living in virtual poverty at our father's home was a safer option than enduring her destructive sociopathic behaviours. During one of our weeding punishments, while we were digging near a neighbour's fence, Jake and I smirked on overhearing their offhand comments. Nancy Neill had told her husband Bill that 'Irate Irene would live until she was over ninety years old, because the devil didn't want his own back'. After repetitively hearing many negative Irate Irene comments, we remained puzzled throughout our lives as to why no churchgoer, neighbour or extended family member had ever intervened to defend us.

I spent most of my life searching for a kind, affectionate

partner possessing the gentle, endearing personality of my dad. A psychologist once explained to me that this goal would be unachievable without counselling. As the oldest sibling, I had very fond memories entrenched in me of my early childhood growing up with my parents, but she explained that I was subconsciously choosing male partners who restored my childhood-distorted concept of the 'normal', aggressive household I grew up in. After being constantly oppressed, the doctor rationalised, I was only attracted to disrespectful, arrogant husbands wanting to dominate me as they satisfied my 'imprinted' concept of normal. In her psychological analysis, the doctor informed me that it was my strong maternal instincts that had left me protecting my three siblings from the age of seven. The psychologist suggested that I was a natural mother to my own seven children, because I was always striving to be a better role model than Irate Irene.

My traumatic experiences with Irate Irene caused me to be conflicted about religion. I could never comprehend how holy values could be so obscenely distorted and manipulated to justify abuse. While raised a Christian, I could never integrate the morals I was taught with the perverse behaviours I was observing. As an adult, I wondered why our minister of religion needed a tenth of our wage every week when we had so many tiny mouths to feed. When my first husband, Danny, left his reliable income to establish a business, we incurred a double mortgage on our house and business that I did not want. Asking our minister for help me to change Danny's mindset was a futile exercise. I was frankly shocked when the misogynist decreed that my role was to 'obey my husband' and 'keep him satisfied in the bedroom'. Did he believe the stork had delivered and cared for all my children?

Our financial difficulties were compounded by unethical clients not paying their bills. However, my attempts to alert my husband that the invoices I was sending out for the business were not being paid led to my being physically and mentally abused. I therefore waited until Danny left for work before packing up the family station wagon to leave town. I had hoped that by creating a distance between myself and Danny, I could keep myself and my children safe. Instead, Danny began tracking my movements through my utility services, the schools the children attended and local churches.

My next partner, Willie Chambers, was a wiry coward who had tried to strangle me from behind while I was leaving him, carrying my two-year-old toddler. It was ironic that both Danny and Willie both became stalkers, menacing me when they could not control my choices. The dishonest Willie even attempted to fraudulently claim ownership of half the vehicle I had purchased before I had met him. Fortunately, both the dealership and receipts I possessed confirmed that I had paid for the van myself from the childcare payments I received when they became available in 1991.

Chapter 6

Chloe

With a career goal to work towards, fate dealt us all another cruel blow. I began detecting subtle cues that my environment was changing, and not in a good way. Initially, I noticed Dad's cough was becoming more constant and he was losing weight. Then there was the unpleasant, purulent smell of old blood and sputum on his breath that seemed to permeate from the soiled tissues my father left in the bathroom bin to his bedside. When I mentioned these concerns to my twenty-one-year-old sister, Vera, who was now married to Danny, I learned our father needed radiation therapy in Brisbane for smoking-related lung cancer. Dad had always rolled up tobacco in cigarette papers without filters, as most did back in the day, as the tailored cigarettes were more expensive. Dad's smoking increased when Mum died. He missed her immeasurably.

In order to alleviate my father's concerns, I reluctantly stayed with Vera and Danny for six weeks while he was hospitalised. In response to the weekly letters I wrote to Dad, I received cards written by his nurse. While these letters portrayed an optimistic picture of a rapid return to good health, nothing was improved on his return home. My anxiety spiralled as I became acutely aware of my father's increasing anorexia, incontinence and fragility. At seventeen years old, having just completed a successful senior high school year, I was devastated to learn that Dad was to be hospitalised and palliated.

Not wanting his children to visit and watch him die as he had witnessed Bella waste away, Dad organised for me to briefly stay with Vera and Danny. As Dad lay dying, feeling defeated and penniless, he never realised that his greatest achievement was the kindness and love that he and Mum had bestowed upon their children. For the Barnett children, the loss of the last person who truly loved them was catastrophic.

Dad's inability to read meant that his will had been signed and read when Mum was still alive. They were very young when they had both directed the Public Curator to sell his estate. The funds from Dad's estate were to be kept in trust until each child was twenty-one-years old. Even when Dad had been originally informed of his chest X-ray diagnosed lung cancer, and his life expectancy maximum of two years, he had optimistically hoped that the therapeutic radiation would delay his demise until we were all more mature.

Rather than prioritising an update of his will immediately

to provide his children a home, Dad had delayed changing the paperwork until he could afford the legal fees. Unfortunately, before Dad realised he was continually deteriorating, he became too breathless to eat or talk. All available energy was diverted towards his struggle for each next breath.

Dad had no sooner died at sixty-nine years before an unethical real estate salesman knocked on the door relentlessly. The Public Curator, motivated by the prospect of a quick sale, had reduced the property value and rapidly placed our attractive property on the market before Dad was even buried, causing the grieving Jake and I profound stress. With our humble house being located in an area featuring spectacular river front and park views zoned for a five-story building, the agents showed more interest in sales commissions than showing any consideration for the two grieving orphans they were rendering homeless.

Converting the property to cash assisted Vera and Danny, who had double mortgages on their house and business. At seventeen, I had just finished my senior year and was not yet earning an income, so Jake relinquished his New South Wales employment and income to return. After the Public Curator had deemed our home an estate, Jake and I needed to pay rent to reside there.

I had been advised at school that I could not register for unemployment benefits under Queensland law until next February. According to the Queensland government, many university students were registering to access unemployment benefits before starting their degrees. Therefore, the government had mandated that those just completing school, intending to seek employment, could not register for three months. With Jake's termination payout needed to fund a bond and pay rent, electricity and food, his money lasted less than a month.

Since no social workers had assisted Dad to ensure the safe custody of his family, neither Jake nor I were aware we were entitled to 'special benefits' until we approached the social services for food. Unable to access our inheritance or Dad's bank accounts, nineteen-year-old Jake and I had only the existing food in the cupboards and meagre rations to live off. However, despite us having to pay rent on our own home, the doorbell was rung constantly by enthusiastic salesmen and buyers.

Despite locking ourselves inside the house to grieve the loss of our father, our privacy was persistently invaded. The Public Curator showed little concern for the displaced children rendered homeless. Unable to procure funds to go to university to pursue my dream of becoming a laboratory scientist, I was forced to go nursing. Nursing provided accommodation and paid training, something I needed as I was totally penniless.

Chapter 7

Chloe

A t 60 kg, I was fair-skinned with dark brown, shoulder-length hair, brown eyes and a sprinkle of freckles scattered on my nose. I adapted to the oppressive nursing hierarchy by socially isolating myself. Entering the hostile nursing profession was parallel with living at Irate Irene's, another sheer nightmare. I found myself again surrounded by intimidating line managers who validated my limited life experiences that people were essentially uncaring. Not willing to be a victim of those keen to exploit or bully me, I withdrew from all friendships and avoided social interaction.

As I began to learn about my adult self, I discovered I possessed a high intelligence, a sound understanding of science and amazing observation skills. From maturing, I eventually learned, after being victimised, that these traits left me anything but powerless. Motivated by the income I was earning, I consciously made choices that allowed me to distance myself from hurtful others. With my rigid walls erected, few people could ingratiate themselves with me. At work, I remained professional, friendly but emotionally distant from the toxic nursing culture. I was purely focused on money for survival. Unlike other more assertive novices, even when forced to work beyond my eight hours unpaid, I always apologised, complied and removed myself from the dysfunctional power gradient as soon as any alleged neglected tasks were completed.

Too used to nobody ever intervening to protect me, I worked many extra unpaid hours, acting like a suppository following the path of least resistance. I remained respectful, polite and totally detached when confronted periodically by obnoxious line managers. While other, more confident novices attempted to challenge the unfair authority figures, I never defended myself with excuses like emergency theatre cases, unplanned admissions or heavy workloads. I despised people too much to want to engage with colleagues, unless it was mandatory. Throughout my life, too many disappointing adults had witnessed the frequent public assaults inflicted on my siblings and me, without anyone ever intervening to protect us. We had learned to survive by trusting no one.

Therefore, even seemingly kind people were considered by Vera, Jake, Georgie and me to be self-serving and avoidable. In my melancholy state, I relied on no one. I learned to make responsible decisions for myself and take few risks. I had no reason to expect that anyone, other than my siblings, would ever help me in any crisis. As an introvert, I had only a two-metre square room to retreat into inside the nurses' quarters, to escape from other happy nursing students eagerly wanting to share a friendship or invitations to social events. Instead, I frugally saved every dollar to afford external rental accommodation, where I could remove myself from the institutional nightmare I existed in. I studied nursing only to maintain my income and to keep poverty at bay. One nurse, Gabby, whom I had not seen since our friendship in primary school, was the exception. Gabby had lived just down the road from us in Gympie with her grandmother during the weekdays while she went to school.

Eventually, I moved out of the nursing quarters with Gabby, only to discover that my new flatmate was constantly bringing home many different male lovers who stayed overnight. With no visitors permitted in the nursing quarters, Gabby's desire for partying was unleashed in our up and downstairs unit. Once again, I found myself confined to a two-metre square room while Gabby partied with her boyfriend and his friends. Gabby's friends always attempted to include me in their fun, but I found the fatigue from studying and working shiftwork was challenging enough. Although I loved the bubbly Gabby, we had grown up to be as different as chalk and cheese.

'Chloe, come to the footy club with us tonight. There's an amazing band playing!'

'No thanks, Gabby. You know, you really need to study three hours a day to get through those next exams, honey,'

I warned. Since I was in the intake of students six months ahead of Gabby, I knew the second-year exams were difficult.

'No! After years of living in the country, I am finally enjoying my freedom with no parents to rein me in,' gloated Gabby.

'Yes, but you need to take studying seriously to keep getting an income, Gabby.'

'No, if you fail an exam, you can always downgrade to an Assistant in Nursing role. I'm not really academic like you.'

'I'm not academic, Gabby. Both my parents died at that hospital. I don't want to kill someone accidentally because I've not done my studies.'

'You double-check every drug every time before you administer it, so how could that happen?'

'Statistically, you get about six hours of concentration in a day. So, the answer is very easy, I'm afraid. You only need to be under slept from night shift or fatigued from eight hours between shifts and it can affect your concentration.'

'You be cautious, Chloe; I'll be happy,' said Gabby provokingly, heading for the door.

So, I lived mainly confined to my bedroom while Gabby entertained visitors. On the few occasions when Gabby and I did go out for a meal, once her friends arrived to drink, I would excuse myself. Three months after we had moved in together, I arrived home to see Gabby sitting quietly in the dark lounge, waiting for me.

'Are you all right, hon?' I asked, acutely aware that silent was not a mode Gabby had ever exhibited.

'You were right – I've failed my second-year exams,' Gabby reported tearfully.

'Oh, I am sorry to hear that.' I hug my solemn colleague. 'What did Matron say?'

'I have to either sit for another exam in a month's time, or I can transfer automatically and enrol as an Assistant in Nursing, using the credits from the subjects that I have passed.'

'What do you want to do? I can help you study if you like. You can use my summaries and I can ask you questions.'

'Book reading bores me,' Gabby replied. 'I think I will just default to AIN.'

'You could end up buggering up your back with years of chronic lifting. Won't you be bored just doing washes, feeds, bed making and incontinence rounds all day?'

'No, as you said, since I don't like studying, it is probably safer for the patients.'

'Yes, but you're a clever girl, Gabby. You're setting yourself up for a hard life, with a lower income.'

'Matron offered me a job in the Central Sterilising Department, cleaning and sanitising instruments all day,' Gabby declares. 'I think I'll take it. Then I won't have to worry about what time I come home.'

'Well, that is better than lifting all the heavy bariatric stroke patients in the medical and rehabilitation wards, I suppose. Are you sure you really want that, though?'

'I should take it while the offer is there ... I guess. If I wait another month and still fail, I could be worse off, as you say.'

'I was trying to warn you, Gabby, not have my concerns

validated. The decisions you make now will impact on your whole future. You need to think about it a bit more then make a careful decision. Maybe write a list weighing up the benefits and risks for each option. There are other choices, too. You could have a second try for the exam, and if the central sterilising job is gone, you could do rehab and medical until you can apply for a job in the outpatient clinics, mental health or somewhere. Take your time hon, think about what you want to be doing twenty years from now. Talk to your Mum and Dad, too.'

'What I need is never to return to remote country life again,' Gabby contemplates. 'I really hated living on the farm with no friends nearby. I was housebound living with Grandma too.'

'Yeah, okay, so you don't want to return home – and you have a job either way – so now it is about which of the jobs you prefer to remain in. If you become a Registered Nurse, you probably will need more training to specialise in whatever field you choose, but it will most likely be easier. You get to focus on study in the area that you are interested in rather than in general training, where every six weeks you are rotated to a new area.'

Gabby accepted the Central Sterilising Department vacancy, without hesitation. Unfortunately, Gabby's reaction to the loss of her career as a Registered Nurse was partying more heavily. Her friends occupied our lounge all hours of the night. The partying only tapered off when Gabby went quiet again, around four months later. I awoke from a night shift to find Gabby tearful and sitting alone in the dark lounge with the vertical blinds drawn.

'Gabby, what's happened?' I asked, astounded.

'I missed my period – the pregnancy kit I bought is positive!'

'Oh hell! What do you want to do? You know I will help you with whatever you decide,' I say, to my distressed flat mate.

'I want to get an abortion. I've been drinking too much ... I'm too young, and Colin and I are not in a relationship.'

'Well, let's get an appointment. I can go with you if you want, when you see the doctor. The first thing will be to make an informed choice. You need to discuss how this termination will happen and whether a termination could affect your ability to carry further pregnancies.'

'Yes! Please come with me, Chloe. I know I've been such a fool. I was taking the pill ... but sometimes I drank so much that I could have vomited it back. A few times, I forgot to take it. Sometimes, there were still pills left over in the packet when I got my period. I have been so depressed, erratic and not paying attention.'

At the end of her appointment, the doctor referred Gabby to the Gynaecologist, Dr Brandon, in the same clinic. Dr Brandon offered Gabby to either take a pill to induce a miscarriage or a dilatation and curettage. Gabby chose the curettage, so that if the abortion pill did not work, she did not become any further advanced with her pregnancy. The same afternoon, after the clinic's sexual health nurse had counselled both Gabby and me as her support person, on the risks of unprotected sex. I held Gabby's hand while the clinic nurse placed her in stirrups for the procedure. During the procedure, Dr Brandon took sexually transmitted disease swabs of Gabby's cervical fluids, which were sent for microscopy, culture and sensitivity for bacterial and viral diseases.

While Dr Brandon injected Gabby's cervix with local anaesthetic, she grimaced intensely and tightened her grip, practically grinding my knuckles to powder. After completing the curettage, I drove Gabby home for a quiet night in with her phone turned off.

'Those local anaesthetic needles were bloody painful,' said Gabby. 'I thought I would at least have been given an oral painkiller.'

'I suppose, since it was at a medical clinic and not a hospital, they do the procedure in a way to encounter as few complications as possible. If they provided narcotics, you would probably have to stay longer, and the cost would have been greater.'

'I know I should be grateful. I am still kicking myself for my own stupidity.'

'It is probably safer after that "sex talk" for you to drink less alcohol and settle down with just the one partner,' I hesitantly suggest. 'There will always be loss in our lives, Gabby. Living a good life is about learning to process loss and grief in healthy ways that allow you to grow from the experience. My dad used to say "that opportunity is disguised as loss". I would not have gone nursing and shared accommodation with you had I gone to university.'

'God! I thought I had left my parents at home!' the stressed Gabby sarcastically responds. 'Sorry for being so blunt, but I'm seriously maxed out today.'

'I care about you, hon. I just don't want you to have to go through all this again. We all make mistakes. The important thing is to process and learn from them, so that we don't repeat the same mistakes again.'

'Well, let's just say, *if* there is a next time, I'll keep some bloody painkillers in my bag and be more prepared. Administering local anaesthetics with no oral painkillers is barbaric. Those needles hurt like hell!'

Gabby's little pixie face with her tiny, upturned nose and vivid blue eyes, looked pale. Her naturally curly, short light brown hair was in disarray. For the first time in the years since I had known her, Gabby was dressed more conservatively than usual. Instead of her brightly coloured, leather, thigh-high skirts and shirts with plunging cleavages, Gabby was wearing long black trousers with a lavender-coloured shirt.

Gabby's next blow was a positive Herpes Simplex Type 2 result from the viral swabs taken during the dilatation and curettage procedure. Gabby did not know who the source of the infection was, since she had not been using condoms. She was also concerned about how many partners she had inadvertently spread the virus to during her promiscuous drinking binges.

'Oh, God,' Gabby sighed in exasperation, 'I don't think I can take much more.'

'Well, hon, at least there are antiviral treatments like acyclovir you can take. Using a condom will also prevent further pregnancies. Even if your partner sees contraceptives in your handbag, just say you don't want to get any sexually transmitted diseases. You do not have to tell anyone that you actually have the herpes virus. Just be careful not to transmit it. Also, the doctor has reassured you that the viral outbreaks should get less frequent as you age.'

'It's like a reality check to tidy up my lifestyle, isn't it?' Gabby said, her sad, blue eyes red-rimmed from crying.

'I think, as the sexual health nurse said, you just need to use condoms and stick to the one partner. It is also safer to be in an exclusive relationship with someone that you care for. It's probably best to be more selective, to find someone that you want to spend every day with and avoid the party guys. Using a condom would also reduce your risk of getting cervical cancer or the virus that causes HIV too. The message you got from your doctor was to take precautions, or it could get more serious.'

'An unwanted pregnancy and this virus are bad enough,' Gabby tearfully replied, dabbing at her sodden eyes.

As I hugged her, Gabby's defeated shoulders shook from crying. Tears intermittently were streaming down her face all evening, even after I tried to distract her with a DVD.

'Why don't you date, Chloe? Timmy is keen to go out with you.'

'I know. He has asked me to go to the cinema. I gently turned him down, Gabby. I told Timmy I had to study. I have only three months until my final exams. I am also too broken, and too bruised, to socialise with anyone. I will always have time for you, Gabby, but I find, generally speaking that people are too hard to deal with. We care for and look after people eight hours a day. I need to come home to peace and quiet, not the demands of a partner. As a vulnerable child, I saw the worst the human race could offer. I was beaten constantly and brutally by a bitch, supposed to be an aunt. My ideal life would be a hermit's life, but who can afford that?'

'But, Chloe, you're kind, caring, smart … You could find a lovely partner.'

'But I don't want to. I enjoy my own company too much – and yours, of course. I find nursing an oppressive profession. Going to work to me is like living in a combat mode for eight hours. There are always nitpicking, nasty and unscrupulous leaders evoking disciplinary measures to abuse their power …'

'Yes, but you could have a pleasant life with someone nice like Timmy who is clever and quiet.'

'I don't want to sound crass, Gabby, but I don't want my body invaded every night. I am going to save up to get a house. I want to save my money, to get away from these eight units full of nurses. I want a loyal puppy or two, not a partner. I genuinely don't like people. They are demanding, exhausting, they generate unnecessary fights … I would enjoy just being left alone. I like you, Gabby, you are a terrific, beautiful friend and I like living with you, but I possess no faith in humanity.

I can tolerate no more pain from vicious people. When we go to work, there is always someone creating unnecessary drama, instigating a witch-hunt on one of their colleagues out of jealousy or spite. I cannot bear the inhumanity.'

'I am sorry that terrible people harmed you when you were young, Chloe, but not everyone wants to hurt you.'

'I know, but I just cannot bear any more cruelty. I honestly don't even want the exhausting effort of trying to separate the good people from the bad. I just want solitude and a pet or two to cuddle. That would be my ideal.'

'You are too young to lock yourself away like a wounded animal. Not everyone wants to exploit or offend you,' Gabby said persistently.

'I understand that you believe that, Gabby. Your experience of growing up on a lovely rural property with devoted parents and a caring grandma who kept you safe and loved would have been wonderful. I am an orphan, so if I got pregnant, there would be no one to help me. To be truly happy, I need to be strong, independent and alone. (You are always excluded from my impression of people, of course.) I am glad we share this unit, you are adorable, but unlike you, I find company tedious.'

'Well, I hope you will not always be distancing yourself from people. I hope lots of kind caring souls surround you, so you do not have to maintain this defensive barrier of alertness around people. I had noticed that at times you looked terribly sad. I did not realise that your melancholy thoughts were from grief.'

'I'm okay. I just have never had any reason to party or celebrate life, like you do.'

'Why don't you come out with our group for a few nights?'

'If I am not studying, I would prefer just to reward myself with a movie and get my uniforms ironed and chores up to date.'

'Yes, but you know our group of friends are very funny. You could enjoy a good laugh.'

'The truth is, Gabby that I would be looking at the door and at my watch constantly, wanting to make my escape. I would honestly feel trapped and forced to wear a plastic smile the whole time. I do not find people or parties at all enjoyable.'

'That's morbid. It's like you don't expect that your life will ever get better!'

'Oh, I do. I am saving up for a deposit for a home and puppy. That is who I am, or what I have become. I am a person who gladly avoids people, along with the physical and emotional pain they intentionally inflict.'

'Well, let's hope that our successful friendship will inspire you to develop more positive relationships down the track to find a lifetime partner,' Gabby optimistically replied. 'I understand that you feel confident helping patients because they are dependent, with less ability to criticise and cause you grief. You are so thoughtful and sensitive, Chloe. You deserve to find a happy mature relationship.'

'Honestly, I find even the idea of that beyond stressful – tiresome!'

Gabby put the kettle on, conscious of the fact that

probably due to her recent vulnerability, this was the first time I had ever opened up to her. The frank conversation had become intense surprisingly quickly. Although I was fragile and timid, Gabby confidently knew that I would never reveal her recent termination or infection to anyone.

Chapter 8

Chloe

E xcitement built in the eight side-by-side units when two of the nurses in unit six got engaged within a month of each other to their long-term partners. Lilly was engaged to a doctor called Flynn, and her flat mate Sheila had become engaged to Brett, a newspaper photographer Gabby and I knew. Most evenings when we arrived home after our evening shifts finished at 11 pm, Gabby or I would escort Brett upstairs so he could walk through my bedroom, along the external fenced verandah, past two units to Sheila's bedroom door.

The hype of the eager nurses heightened as the date for Lilly and Flynn's wedding drew near. Both Lilly and Sheila were so immersed in choosing wedding and bridesmaid's dresses, booking venues, floral arrangements, honeymoon destinations and music bands that no one was prepared for the devastation that hit.

As flatmates, Sheila and Lilly intended to be bridesmaids for each other, with their weddings planned six months apart. Many of the nurses sharing the units in the building were requesting the wedding dates off well in advance of the rosters being completed, to ensure they could attend both celebrations. However, Sheila's excitement waned when, at Brett's buck's party, he overindulged drinking beers and tripped down three steps, breaking his right arm. The next blow for Sheila was Brett losing his job after his dominant arm was encased in a plaster cast for months. Sadly, Brett's unemployment triggered a reactive depression, and he began drinking more to alleviate his low mood.

Lilly and Flynn were married first, with Sheila and Brett being the Matron of Honour and Best Man respectively. Shortly after the marriage ceremony, Brett was drinking heavily during the photo shoot. When Brett vomited and was unable to protect his airway, Flynn placed Brett in the recovery position. However, with Brett's conscious level diminishing, he inevitably inhaled his own vomit. As the ambulance arrived, Flynn attempted to place a breathing tube into Brett's lungs. The breathing tube soon filled with the undigested food, being expelled from Brett's over-distended stomach. When a paramedic also attempted to intubate Brett's airway, the stomach acid entered his lungs, producing life-threatening bronchospasms. At thirty years old, Brett died from asphyxia in the Emergency Department. At Sheila's insistence, Lilly and Flynn had still gone on their two-week Hawaiian honeymoon. Flynn and Lilly were unable to console the mortified Sheila. All the nurses in our units were horrified by how quickly their wedding celebration had spiralled into such an unmitigated disaster.

During her grieving, I kept an eye on Sheila, bringing her food and often offering her a lift to work on days when she felt so sad she would not have got out of bed without gentle coaxing. With Gabby drinking heavily again after Brett's death, I often simply held Sheila and listened as she sobbed, recalling fond memories of her fiancé. I patiently helped Sheila, at a pace she could tolerate, to cancel their wedding venue bookings, honeymoon reservations and eventually return Brett's belongings to his grief-stricken family.

By simply being my kind, compassionate self, I had unwittingly bonded with another friend, broadening my limited social sphere. When Sheila observed the turmoil Gabby's binge drinking was having on my ability to study and sleep after shiftwork, she offered me one of the keys to the upstairs bedroom that she and Brett had previously occupied. Sheila had moved all her belongings into Lilly's old bedroom to escape her memories. Exchanging our spare keys also provided the extra security that Sheila needed, should she accidentally lock herself out.

After graduating to become a Registered Nurse, Sheila decided she could afford not to share her unit again. By keeping her old room vacant, except for the odd night that I escaped Gabby's partying friends, Sheila felt she needed solitude to re-evaluate her disrupted future plans.

On learning from their parents that Sheila was now living alone, her older brother, Keith, a grader driver currently working in the area, also intended visiting on his occasional weekends off while doing roadwork at Kilkivan. Since Keith had been previously working on road works at Theodore, Eidsvold and Gayndah, she had not seen him for months. Sheila was delighted when Keith had rung, asking to visit for the Easter long weekend.

Chapter 9

Keith

Thus, for the first time in six months, Sheila giggled hysterically. She found Chloe and me, total strangers to each other, in her old bed the next morning. Not wanting to wake my sister up, I had used the unit keys she had provided on a previous fleeting visit to let myself in. I arrived late after a frustrating day, where intermittent showers had delayed the road work we were trying to complete before the long weekend. After eating during my drive to Gympie, I arrived around 10.30 pm, showered and fell asleep promptly on my back.

I awoke, totally bewildered. A warm female was in my arms, wrapped around me, breathing softly. What had woken me was the odd sensation of drool trickling onto my chest and the weight of her head and arm on my shoulder. On hearing Sheila wandering out of her bedroom, I quietly hissed 'Sis!', hoping to attract her attention to get assistance in extricating myself from the embrace of this amorous stranger. However, on seeing my predicament, Sheila had laughed uncontrollably. With her eyes bright and amused, Sheila placed her hand over her mouth to muffle her giggles before dashing off to the loo to relieve her full bladder. She was absolutely no help at all. Worst still, when Sheila returned, looking at the totally relaxed lady, she instructed me to lie still and not disturb her.

'Chloe's from unit four,' whispered my entertained sister.

'What's she doing here?' I whispered, feeling totally embarrassed at this predicament.

'Chloe's flat mate, Gabby, is a party animal, so I gave her a key to the bedroom balcony door for when she needed to get some sleep here.'

Apparently, according to my sister, Chloe hardly ever came over. It was only when she was exhausted from shiftwork and study that she arrived during the night if Gabby's company got too noisy.

'Lift her arm up for me,' I whispered.

'No! She'll wake up.'

'I need to get up.'

'No, you don't!'

'Sheila, you stop this! You get here right now!' I demanded, blushing from awkwardness.

'Chloe didn't bring her alarm clock and uniform, so she must be on a day off.'

'You're no bloody help!' I hoarsely whispered in frustration. 'Get back here, you little witch!'

'Enjoy the attention,' replied my thoroughly entertained sister, leaving me imprisoned.

I was instantly relieved when Sheila returned, until I saw why! While we had always teased each other mercilessly, I had not imagined that Sheila's only response would be to arrive back in the bedroom to record my vulnerability on her phone camera. With my left side weighed down by the sleeping Chloe, I had raised my right fist and clenched my teeth, silently warning my sister to stop. However, the expression of disapproval on my face only humoured rather than deterred the exuberant Sheila.

'Now give me a nice smile for Mum and Dad,' teased Sheila as she clicked away.

'Don't you bloody dare!'

'Come on, be a sport. It isn't often your helplessness gets as good as this!' Sheila smiled as she excitedly clicked away.

'When I get out of this, you little minx, I'm letting every one of your tyres down,' I warned, attempting to discourage Sheila's clicking.

'How about a smile for Chloe?' Sheila provoked.

'I was going to take you out for lunch today, but you don't bloody well deserve it!' I whisper furiously, as the phone camera clicks again.

A few bips and Sheila looked at her incoming texts, grinning widely.

'Mum and Dad want to know who the cutie is, and how serious is your relationship.'

Sheila texted back.

'What are you telling them, you brat?' I couldn't help laughing. It had been ages – since Brett's death, really – since I had seen Sheila looking this cheerful.

'Not much. I'm just reassuring them they might not have such a long wait for grandchildren after all,' Sheila chuckled.

'This is supposed to be your friend, Sheila. Think about her reputation,' I added seriously.

'Thinking about some nephews and nieces is more pleasurable,' Sheila eagerly replied.

'I just woke up like this,' I pleaded innocently. 'She was not here when I arrived. I went to bed alone in this dark room!'

'Yes, I hung darker curtains for night duty. Chloe liked them too, so I left them there.'

I lay there trapped, while my vibrant sister enjoyed her payback.

'What time is it?' I queried.

'Just after 7 am,' Sheila commented after checking the time on her phone. 'Chloe probably tried to sleep at her place until about two or three. She would have come through the other entrance and crashed, not realising you were here. She'll probably only need another few hours.'

'You stop that right now!' I pointed my right hand at Sheila and her phone.

'I might not get such an opportunity with you again,' Sheila laughed softly. 'I'm obliged to make the most of it.'

'When she wakes up, I am going to pretend that I'm asleep. You are going to let her leave here and say nothing, do you hear me?'

'Look how cute this one looks,' taunted Sheila, showing me an image of Chloe's sheer white satin nightie. 'I might need that pic as a screensaver.'

I smiled, shaking my head, unable to help myself. That image was really cute. The truth was that I wouldn't mind a copy of that picture myself. Chloe's long, dark brown hair was draped over my shoulder and my left arm was along her back, almost to her bottom. Chloe's left arm was folded over my waist. This Chloe looked so adorable that I had to admit to myself I found her intimate contact entirely agreeable. I did not mind being unable to move. I lay there, enjoying Chloe's unguarded touch, sincerely hoping that she did not wake up with a fright. All I could do was elevate my arm, so that when she did move, it was not still entangling me.

Chloe's eyes were blissfully shut. Her face and body looked totally relaxed, as her gaping rose mouth dribbled more saliva onto my chest. I noticed just a hint of cleavage was visible above the white satin nightdress, as the warm Chloe kicked off the doona. At least Sheila had mopped up the drool that was beginning to flow without disturbing Chloe's slumber, while strategically leaving her phone out of reach.

Sheila warned me now in all seriousness. 'You better pretend to be asleep when Chloe wakes up. Chloe tends to be a bit of a loner, she doesn't date, so this is actually a bit of a dilemma. I know you have been a gentleman, but Chloe won't know that. If Chloe does not wake up enough for you to extricate yourself, just pretend you are asleep and oblivious to her being here.'

'Don't you worry about that! As far as I am concerned, *this* did not happen,' I warned, pointing to the sleeping Chloe. 'And don't you dare send those photos to anyone!'

'I haven't,' confessed Sheila. 'That text was just Gabby checking to see if Chloe was here.'

Sheila tilted her head, taking a final look at Chloe and me approvingly before leaving. I had the sneaking suspicion that Sheila was contemplating the intriguing possibility of a romance between me and the shy Chloe. I was single, so why not? I would love to be a partner to this little cutie.

While teasing me, I worried that Sheila had not missed the fleeting expression of attraction my face may have revealed, when she showed me that appealing photo. I was enjoying this intimate moment with Chloe immensely. Her skin felt so soft, warm and smooth.

Chapter 10

Sheila

Chloe had consistently refused to socialise with any of our nursing colleagues, even the night of her graduation to become a Registered Nurse. While I loved the shy Chloe, I could not help but notice that she was fragile. Yet, she had been the first person to offer assistance when I had returned alone to my flat after Brett's death at Lilly's wedding. Brett had often remarked about how he was surprised that Chloe was still single, when she let him into her flat to walk along the balcony above the carport to my room. Chloe had spent most of the weekend with me after Brett's funeral, making sure I was okay.

There were many nights when Chloe had hugged me as I wept loudly, recalling the life I had planned with Brett. While most of the other nurses had returned to their normal lives, the sensitive Chloe had spent a lot of time with me. We had bought groceries together. Chloe had ironed my uniforms, put a load of washing on, brought over cooked meals and calmly listened as I poured out my grief. There was no judgement from Chloe. Chloe had gently reminded me about the wedding venue and honeymoon bookings that needed to be cancelled, helping me gradually get my lonely life back on track, one small step at a time. When I felt fragmented and immobilised with despair, the reassuring Chloe was always there. Chloe had answered the door, fielded phone calls about funeral arrangements and worked between Brett's parents and me, helping us to pick favourite photos for the eulogy. She had even helped me select a handsome photo for the headstone.

That was why I had offered Chloe the spare room key, to help her get some quiet relief from Gabby's binge drinking and partying. I had caught Chloe placing a lock on the inside of her bedroom door after one of Gabby's drunken friends had wandered in uninvited. Chloe needed somewhere to retreat to when Gabby was being less considerate than her usual self.

Unfortunately, it was not long before Gabby's reckless behaviour resulted in another unwanted pregnancy. Gabby told me about her crisis, not Chloe. Chloe had only asked me to swap a few shifts after Gabby had called in sick. Chloe had maintained Gabby's privacy on both occasions. It was only when Gabby had apologised to me for the inconvenience of all the shift changes Chloe had negotiated that I had understood how much Chloe was struggling. Although

Chloe was concerned that Gabby was making 'poor choices' as a reaction to her demotion to Assistant in Nursing, her loyalty had never wavered. The protective Chloe supported Gabby through her second abortion, without judging her carelessness or irresponsibility.

I had silently observed Gabby's dilemma from a distance, noting how Chloe was comforting us both during our individual upsets without judging or gossiping. Chloe looked so relaxed and unguarded in my brother's arms that I was pleased Keith had allowed her that well-earned rest. I was pleased when Keith planned to feign sleep, if Chloe did not roll over to release them from that compromising situation. How would Chloe deal with this predicament if she ever learned about it, I wondered.

Chapter 11

Chloe

Vera had coped with our turbulent childhood by attempting to protect Jake, Georgie and I from Irate Irene. However, in being a martyr to us, she had become a victim herself. Vera's confidence at school, at church and in her friendships waned. Vera found herself flailing at every protective strategy she employed. Devoting herself to religion and precarious relationships produced more dire circumstances. At one stage, Vera had landed on my doorstep abruptly with no food and three children, after leaving the abusive Danny.

With customers absconding and not paying for his labour, their church still demanded a tenth of his income. With Vera unwilling to take contraceptives, Danny was heading for financial ruin. Unwilling to take responsibility for his aggression, Danny tried to rationalise his assault. Rather than regret leaving his paid employment, Danny blamed his financial strain on the stress of a minister not permitting him to reduce his church contributions and an 'inflexible' wife rigidly refusing to obey his wishes.

Vera abruptly left their house the next morning, packing up all the children's belongings after Danny went to work. She left Danny with a desolate house. After that one impulsive act, Danny would rarely get access to their children again. If Danny closed down his business and booked a motel in Brisbane after a four-hour drive to access his legal weekend of custody, he would discover that Vera had either left town for the day or had again changed addresses without notifying him. Vera's reaction to his assault was to maintain total control over her children, leaving Danny unable to maintain any contact with them.

Determined to keep her children safe, Vera changed the children's surnames after their divorce without Danny's permission. Vera registered their children in schools under her new husband's surname then changed her phone numbers as frequently as her addresses. Vera would not pick up the phone if she identified his number on caller ID. With seven children, Vera's social security benefits increased considerably, allowing her to purchase a larger family car. The different vehicle registration in her new married name also increased Danny's difficulty locating their children.

Vera's next partner, the quick-tempered Willie, had two children from his previous marriage. Willie also assaulted Vera when she attempted to leave by trying to strangle her from behind as she walked away from their house, carrying her toddler. In his uncontrolled fury, Willie was charged with a second assault of a police officer. However, that did not deter Willie from threatening me when I provided accommodation for my sister and her children.

'I know where you live,' Willie menaced, when seeing me getting groceries at my corner store.

'Oooh! I'm sure my cousin in the police force will find you without any bother, if you come near us. The Criminal Investigation Bureau will have your history of felonies on file,' I loudly replied, storming past him.

'You just wait!' called Willie, shaking his fist angrily, as I continued walking to my vehicle.

'You come around looking for trouble? You won't go away disappointed!' I shouted, fed up with Willie's menacing. 'Everyone, please notify the police that you have witnessed William Chambers threatening me,' I shouted to onlookers, to expose his behaviour.

Willie clearly needed reminding that actions have consequences. By using recommended public exposure to stop bullying, I was demonstrating that I would not be intimidated. However, instead of feeling humiliated, Willie immediately attempted to pursue me until several males stepped forward to intervene.

Thwarted in his efforts, Willie shouted, 'You'll keep', before returning to his vehicle. Relieved, I exhaled forcefully before returning my trolley to the bay.

On witnessing this public spectacle, Keith Johnson was

concerned to recognise me, Sheila's friend, Chloe, being threatened. He took intentionally large strides towards the wiry shorter offender to distract his attention away from me.

'I won't mind helping you on your way either, sunshine,' Keith shouted in a demeaning tone.

Totally embarrassed at the turn of events, Willie scrambled into his small blue sedan, keen to be seen heading in the opposite direction.

Chapter 12

Georgie

A year after Vera left Irate Irene's, Jake accepted a salesman role with a large firm offering to relocate him to New South Wales. Jake only returned to Gympie on hearing that our father had lung cancer and had been hospitalised for terminal care. Jake took leave of absence until his employer found a position vacant in Gympie so he could care for our younger sister, Chloe, now seventeen years old. I had left school at fifteen years and joined the Air Force. I desperately needed to escape the malicious Irene, who lacked any concept of a healthy parental relationship. Following my recruitment, I was only able to return to the Barnett home for a week to see my father and attend his funeral.

I became trapped in the Air Force on a three-year contract when my Uncle Ross, as guardian, had refused his permission to allow me to leave. Since I was underage, the Air Force

Warrant Officer had discussed my request for discharge with my guardians in my absence. Without my consent, all parties then made an autocratic decision requiring me to remain enlisted for the duration of my contract. After six months, I had had a gutful of the military bastardisation process. The intake of novices I was in had been subjected to parades where we were required to dress in uniform, all hours of the day and night, when a fire alarm sounded. The Air Force had lost its appeal after our group of recruits had had our car tyres deflated, been forced to clean the bathrooms with toothbrushes and endured dehumanising insults from senior staff. I felt betrayed when my wishes were ignored by the RAAF's senior officers and supported by my supposed next of kin. I learnt the hard way never to put anyone other than Jake, Vera or Chloe down as my next of kin ever again.

Leaving the RAAF without permission would see me detained on criminal charges, I was warned. With the systematic bullying, I felt no safer than I had been at Irate Irene's, where the odd, unpredictable beating without any reason had left me hyper-alert and traumatised. When I found myself attracted to a tall, leggy, wavy-haired blonde with an olive complexion, I had not anticipated that my distorted concept of a normal relationship would result in marital disharmony. With the Air Force relocating us every two years, my wife, Brooke, with no driver's licence and a poor education after childhood illnesses, struggled to adapt to each new environment. Initially determined to do evening courses to achieve a higher education to qualify with a computing degree to join civilian life, I ended up stuck with military life. Brooke needed to get groceries, find local doctors and attend to household maintenance, as our three young children were occupying most of her days.

A major problem in my marriage was that Brooke and I also had different philosophies on living. Brooke lived exclusively in the present. In contrast, I was investing time and energy to make elaborate plans that would get me out of the RAAF as soon as possible. We argued a lot, as Brooke showed no interest in wanting to comprehend my long-term investment goals. At the time, with the inexperience of youth, I had naively failed to realise how unrealistic my ambitions were with a young family. When my finances kept me dependent on remaining in the RAAF, I did many self-development courses trying to find happiness and learn assertive behaviours. I even tried to live economically, determined to retire early from the unyielding military attitudes, the demoralising leadership and dysfunctional power games which replicated my unhappy, unsafe childhood.

Like my siblings, I limited my interaction with others by intentionally withdrawing from society and friends. While I enjoyed travelling and playing musical instruments, nothing else seemed to have the same soothing effects as conversations with family members. Throughout my life, I found other people left me agitated. In particular, when interacting socially with work colleagues or churchgoers, I found their poor decisions, emotional turmoil, unsound logic and a tendency to generate dramas all too familiar.

Chapter 13

Irene and her children

Grandchildren coming to visit were never a problem experienced by Irate Irene. Most of her children had left town for university and never returned. Five of Irate Irene's children were ever only heard of when she boasted of their accomplishments to churchgoers, unable to diplomatically make a hasty retreat. Irene's 'children should be seen and not heard' mentality left most parishioners visibly cringing. Too many could recall the bruises and flesh wounds Irate Irene had inflicted upon the vulnerable Barnett children. 'Never spare the rod and spoil the child', Irene would proudly decree when boasting of the lawyer, accountant, college professor, engineer and doctor she felt responsible for inspiring towards success.

Even the church minister, whose intrinsic belief was that everyone possessed good, only considered Irate Irene useful as an organ donor. Irene was rarely notified of church meetings and fundraisers. If she attended any events, it was due to conversations overheard rather than any personal invitations.

On one occasion, Irene had discovered from gossip in the toilet stalls that her daughter, Joy, had been hospitalised to have a bowel cancer resected. Unfortunately, Joy and Margaret were the only family members still residing in town. Irene's first dysfunctional power game was demanding custody of her reluctant grandchildren from her son-in-law, Paul. After Paul's attempts to pacify Irene were futile, the four-year-old twins, Troy and Tony, had to stay one afternoon with their grandmother. Naturally, both twins were returned to Paul in tears after Irene had told them they were selfish for asking to visit their hospitalised mother during her recovery. Joy's response was to ensure that she was independently mobile when Irene visited, whether it was in hospital or at home.

After Joy was released from hospital, Paul set up a bed in the back room of their business, predominantly to ensure that no one would be home if Irene and Ross visited. The twins could play in the back room while Joy rested in peace. Paul would then order takeaway meals to collect on the way home. Even if Joy wasn't well before a visit from Irene, she was sure to maintain the façade of mobilising with a good posture and acting as though she was boosting with energy. Paul would warn Joy if he saw his mother-in-law arriving and hurriedly rush the twins into their room to play. Paul would then start up the noisy vacuum cleaner to drown out her foghorn, demoralising comments.

For Paul Carter, the presence of the destructive Irene had cured him of any desire of a kinship relationship for life. Paul had heard Irate Irene's opinion on every aspect of their wedding plans from her disapproval of Joy's beautiful, white, lacy wedding dress, her criticisms of the professionally decorated wedding cake, their honeymoon destination and of course, the groom not being good enough for her youngest daughter. In fact, Paul's parents attempting to defend their son's reputation were left in disbelief at Irene's arrogance and rudeness.

'That stupid woman has no boundaries,' Paul's father complained to his son.

'Just keep the peace for this one day, please, Dad. Hopefully, you will never have to see her again,' Paul whispered in his father's ear.

'I want that in writing, son! She has no respect for either of you, to be trying to ruin your wedding day like this.'

'That was not a special performance, Dad. That is Irate Irene, every day! You should feel sorry for Joy. She has had to live with that hideous excuse for a parent most of her life.'

'Well, I must say Joy has my deepest sympathy.'

'Sympathy for what?' questioned Ross, overhearing Paul's father's comment.

'I was just telling Dad how Joy had to make many of the wedding arrangements several times, like when the florists did not write the orders down clearly,' Paul replied, recovering swiftly.

Right on cue, Joy's brother, David, arrived. Joy had

begged her brother to keep their mother away from Paul's family. When David had asked Joy for suggestions about a wedding gift, Joy's main request was the need for him to run interference to protect the guests from their dogmatic, opinionated mother. A deal was struck.

David attempted to buffer guests from the impact of Irene, while Paul spent the $100 David gave his brother-in-law to purchase a souvenir of their honeymoon. Paul was left in no doubt as to who got the better end of that deal! While Joy's siblings would have liked to attend her wedding to spend time with their father, even the thought of sharing any conversations with their embarrassing mother was too humiliating. Other than Ross possessing a kind nature, no one ever understood why he had chosen such a miserable wife as a mother for his children.

'People place themselves where they think they need to be,' a psychologist had explained to David, when he had asked that very question about his father during a counselling session. David had asked the professional's advice about how to manage his mother's behaviours. David had informed the psychologist that while he wanted to maintain a relationship with his even-tempered father, he found his mother beyond intolerable. Basically, David was advised that while his parents remained married, he should limit his relationship with his father to phone calls from a distance. The only other recommendation was 'not to reward undesirable behaviours with attention' or they would be repeated.

'That would be all of my mother's behaviours,' David

had alleged. 'She would not know how to treat anyone with respect or compassion. All my life, she has lacked social awareness.'

Irene's repertoire of conversations, which constantly compared her family with others, were always malicious. Worse still, in the middle of a rant where Irene demanded everyone's attention, she could never be stopped. Irene could evacuate a room within five minutes of her presence, which was a feat, especially at joyous family occasions like weddings and christenings. Typically, Ross would attempt to distract Irene's condemnations by diverting her attention to other pleasant sights, only for her to embark on another tirade that only he was left to listen to.

Chapter 14

Keith's hospital visit

The moment Chloe rolled onto her other side, Keith tentatively climbed out of bed. He collected his clothes and shoes then quietly tiptoed downstairs. Blissfully unaware of her nocturnal bonding, Chloe awoke around 9.15 am. She neatly remade the queen-size bed before exiting from the bedroom door along the balcony to her own unit. Grossly mortified by the predicament he had found himself in Keith could neither relax, nor enjoy the humour in Sheila's teasing until Chloe had returned to her own flat.

Keith planned to sleep on the sofa the following night, even after Sheila had informed him that Chloe rarely stayed over two nights in a row. Sheila's calm demeanour did not mollify Keith's scepticism. Eventually, to appease him, Sheila knocked on Chloe's door to announce that her brother had just arrived and was staying for the weekend in her old bedroom. Sheila's sense of fun was further ignited when Chloe's innocent expression revealed no awareness of Keith's previous captivity in her embrace.

On Sheila's return to her unit, Keith was so keenly interested in Chloe's response that he did not realise he was holding his breath until a huge sigh of relief escaped his pursed lips. Sheila's mirth warned Keith his sister would be dining out on this misadventure for some time to come. Keith's mouth curled up at the corners, as he shook his head vigorously to discourage her.

All Saturday, every phone ping had been Keith's matchmaking sister sending him more images of his Chloe encounter. Shooting Sheila a sideways look, in his deep voice, Keith said, 'Enough!' However, as usual, Keith's contagious smile diluted his serious intent, making Sheila's infectious laugh erupt once again. It was bad enough that the images of Chloe's warm embrace were crystallised in his memory and secretly saved onto his phone without his mischievous sister joyfully reminding him of the intimate moment.

'I'm hoping that was just a test drive,' remarked his giggling sister.

Sheila began thinking of ways that she could introduce Keith and Chloe without her friend becoming suspicious of her intentions. The means of an introduction came in the most unexpected manner. Jill, another nursing friend of Chloe's and Sheila's, visited Chloe after Gabby left for her evening shift. Jill needed a 'light and shade' picture, to complete her photography assignment. While they were waiting for their dinner to cook on the stove, Jill talked Chloe into wearing her bikini to model the grass skirt and grass bra souvenir that Lilly and Flynn had brought back from their honeymoon. Taking directions from Jill, Chloe climbed onto the corner of the railings at the top of the stairs at the back of her unit. Jill was halfway down the stairs, paying attention to the lighting on Chloe's face, when the evening breeze abruptly blew the door shut.

Hence, to Sheila's utter delight, the shocked Keith had answered the door when Jill and the half-naked Chloe had knocked to borrow their unit's spare key, to rescue their meal still cooking on the stove.

Keith was rendered so speechless that it was left to Sheila to invite them both in. Sheila spontaneously erupted with laughter, when Chloe immediately went to her linen cupboard to borrow a towel to wrap over her bikini. Taken by surprise, the stunned Keith maintained eye contact with the beetroot-red Chloe. Beyond amused, Sheila tactfully introduced both nurses to her older brother. Chloe's smile masked her feelings of dread, as she modestly covered her exposed tanned flesh. Jill, too, was smiling at their dilemma, as she explained the technical aspects of her photography assignment.

'Did you end up getting the picture snapped?' asked Sheila, keen to see the result.

'Yes, just the one, right before the door slammed,' Jill said. Keen to legitimise Chloe's attire, Jill placed the snapshot on the screen for Sheila to scrutinise.

'That looks lovely, Chloe', Sheila remarked, passing the image over to Keith. With the towel secured in place, Chloe looked over at the screen, steadying it. She unconsciously moved close enough to give Keith goose bumps from her breath on the back of his neck. Following Jill's instructions, Chloe was innocuously looking up at the sun, with each arm firmly gripping the corner rails behind her for support. Dangling from Chloe's pink, painted toenails were the matching grass slippers with the same tiny flower borders featured on the grass skirt waist and bra. Jill had placed a hibiscus flower in Chloe's hair behind her ear to complement the breathtaking image. The combined effects of the beautiful photograph, Chloe's proximity and her lovely floral fragrance left Keith squirming. Sheila, recognising the telltale signs of her brother's discomfort, was immeasurably encouraged.

'I did nothing,' defended the amused Sheila, widening her arms in a plea after they had left. 'You were the one answering the door.'

Sheila innocently smiled, when her brother locked his gaze on her animated face.

'You look far too pleased with yourself. Please don't, sis. I like Chloe. Don't chase her away from me,' Keith pleaded earnestly.

'So, you admit you are interested in Chloe, then?'

'Yes, but if anything happens between us, let it occur naturally. No matchmaking, sis!'

Later on, shortly after their evening meal, Keith began gripping his right lower abdomen and grunting. As Sheila tried to assist him to walk to her car, another wave of searing pain caused Keith to bend over and vomit spontaneously.

Apologising profusely while still gripping his side, his face blanched into a greyish colour. Sheila found an empty blue ice cream dish for any further vomit before assisting her stooping brother to return to the nearby lounge. Shaken by his appearance, Sheila's instincts were to call an ambulance. However, Keith insisted his pain was rapidly dissipating.

'We need to get you to the hospital and assessed,' asserts Sheila.

'I'll be all right, sis. I am sorry about that awful mess. I can't clean it up right now, but I will.'

'I'm not worried about the mess. You don't look right,' Sheila said, looking anxious.

'Just hang back,' Keith grunted 'I've had this dull ache in my side coming and going for a few days. Eating something just stirred it up again. It'll settle.'

'A few days? Why didn't you say anything?'

'I've probably just eaten something that didn't agree with me,' Keith said, minimising his distress. 'That pain seems to be easing off slightly now.'

'Well, you still need to get that checked out. Have you been eating properly? Have your bowels moved every day?' Sheila asked.

'Mind your business, sis. You're getting *waaaay* too personal!'

'No, it's important. Answer my questions. Before tonight, when did you last eat?'

'Friday night, on the drive here. I bought a toasted ham, tomato and cheese sandwich. But I only ate about a quarter, before I started feeling squeamish.'

'So, you had nothing else today except for what you've just vomited?'

'No, just water. That was all I felt like. I'll come good. Just a bug, probably.'

'Was anyone else on the site sick?'

'No, not that I know of.'

'And when was your last poo?'

Sheila wanted to look at his abdomen, but Keith kept instinctively protecting his right side, pushing her hands away.

'Thursday, but as I said, I have not been eating.'

'Poke out your tongue.'

'What?'

'Poke out your tongue!'

'Sis, just leave me, please. I feel a bit off, that's all. I'm not up to party tricks.'

'I just want to see your tongue,' Sheila persisted.

Keith poked out his tongue; it was brown coated, validating he was mildly dehydrated. He was still guarding his right side and umbilicus area, defensively pushing his sister's hands away, worried that Sheila might trigger further attacks of pain.

'Okay, we are going to try again to get you into the car. We need to go to the hospital. I suspect you have appendicitis.'

'Seriously, sis, I'm fine.'

'When I pushed here, you got pain on the other side of

your abdomen, Keith. That's called rebound tenderness. You most likely have a grumbling appendix.'

As Keith attempted to stand, another intense searing pain gripped his side, causing him to grunt, brace and hold his breath. Keith buckled over again, almost falling before Sheila steadied him back onto the lounge. Sheila rang the ambulance, reporting his 8/10 right-sided iliac fossa pain.

In the hospital, Keith's laboratory tests revealed an extremely raised white cell count and elevated C reactive protein, validating inflammation was present. The bedside ultrasound performed due to Keith's labile blood pressure suggested a gangrenous appendix.

Intravenous fluids were commenced for rehydration, while he was prepared for surgery. Keith awoke several hours later in the intensive care unit with a central line imbedded into his chest, delivering noradrenaline to treat his septic shock. Keith put his hand up automatically to investigate his tender nose. He discovered it was sore from the nasogastric tube inserted into his right nostril which was travelling down to his stomach. Keith's awareness of the tube irritating the back of his throat began making him gag. Seeing the greenish bile draining from the tube hanging out his nose triggered another retching movement, as Keith braced his surgical wound in pain.

'Keith, you need to lie really still,' Chloe, his ICU nurse, softly instructed, as she looked down from setting his monitor parameters. 'The more you move, the more the tube will mechanically stimulate the back of your throat. If you can lie really still for me, I can get you some pain relief.'

Keith nods slowly, trying to remain as still as possible. 'I feel sick, but I'm too scared to vomit. It will hurt too much.'

'Okay, well, lie still and I'll get you something for the nausea, too. You are unlikely to vomit, because that tube in your nose has emptied your stomach,' Chloe assured him.

Not recognising the pale, dishevelled Keith, Chloe administered small doses of narcotics and an anti-emetic medication while watching his vital signs on the monitor. Chloe began titrating his intravenous noradrenaline infusion with the narcotics she was administering intravenously, until his pain subsided.

'You will go to sleep soon, Keith. Before you do, I just need you to take some deep breaths. I'd like you to inflate your ribs at the bottom of your lungs, so that my hands move,' Chloe said, leaning over placing both hands on his lower rib cage on both sides. 'Every time you wake up, I need you to take ten more deep breaths for me. The deep breaths are necessary to reduce your risk of a chest infection after the anaesthetic and pain relief.'

Keith inhaled, deeply stimulated by Chloe's pleasant floral scent invading his left patent nostril. Keith found himself appreciating that professional Chloe dressed in navy scrubs was just as sexy as one wearing the white satin nightie in his bed.

'Is my sister still waiting for me in the Emergency Department?' asked Keith, attempting to distract his mind from the soft warm hands that had been splayed on his ribs bilaterally.

'Oh, I'm not sure. What's her name? I will ring down and

check,' said Chloe, looking at her watch. 'You have been in theatre for about three hours, so she could be still in the surgical waiting room.'

Seeing Keith struggling to talk from his dry mouth, Chloe added, 'Would you like to try some ice chips to suck? The ice will help to moisten your mouth and numb the area where the tube is irritating the back of your throat too.'

After Keith nodded, Chloe returned with a glass of crushed ice, placing a teaspoon full onto Keith's dry, coated tongue. While using the cordless phone to ring the surgical ward, Chloe opened Keith's chart, looking for his surname to ask for his sister. As Sheila's image appeared on the ICU external door camera, Chloe finally realised that Keith was her friend's brother.

Chloe opened the ICU door by depressing the magnetising button, reassuring Sheila that Keith's blood pressure and vital signs had stabilised.

Chloe looked on as Keith smiled to disarm Sheila's worried expression. Sheila sat, holding her brother's hand before whispering something in his ear. Witnessing their familiar camaraderie, Chloe reflectively wished that she had experienced such closeness with her own siblings, whom she had not heard from in months. Watching Sheila tease and taunt her brother to elicit combative responses, Chloe experienced a pang of envy.

As she prepared to give Keith the post-operative wash required to remove the Betadine that was painted on to decontaminate his skin prior to surgery, mischief was written all over Sheila's face. Chloe began to feel uneasy.

'Would you prefer one of the other nurses look after Keith?' Chloe sensitively queried. 'I'm sorry, I did not realise the patient I was allocated was your brother.'

'No, no, absolutely not! I have just been teasing my brother about his vomiting back my seafood pizza,' said Sheila, smiling. 'Keith always tells me my cooking is a lethal weapon. Now this just proves it! You're happy with Chloe looking after you, aren't you, Keith?'

'Of course. She has been amazing, except for letting terrorists in, that is', Keith smiles, nodding towards his sister. 'I've been in safe hands, sis.'

'Well, I will leave Chloe to give you your wash. Will I bring up some toiletries and pyjamas in the morning?'

'Yes, thanks, sis. Oh, and my phone charger, pretty please. You probably need to ring Mum and Dad too. Make sure you tell them I'm fine, though.'

Sheila leant forward to kiss Keith's forehead, keen not to disturb any tubes. Keith braced suddenly then lifted the sheets, identifying the source of his pain. 'Oh my God, sis! They've stuck another tube in my dick,' the horrified Keith announced.

'Keith, your gangrenous appendix is out, but we now have to wait for the antibiotics to work. The only way we can make sure that your kidney and other internal organs are getting enough blood flow is to measure that your kidneys are producing enough urine per hour. If that tube tells us that you are producing less than 40 ml of pee an hour, we need to increase the noradrenaline or give you more intravenous fluids. We adjust that infusion to increase your blood pressure. The kidneys are called the "windows to the viscera" because if they get enough blood flow to make enough urine, then the rest of your organs are getting enough blood flow too,' Chloe explained.

'Oh God, that tube is soooo uncomfortable.'

'I can put some numbing gel around the tube for comfort, if you want. However, the main thing is to just try to relax your muscles, to let the tube drain. Don't try to pee like you normally would, as the urine is emptying automatically into this bag.'

Chloe showed him his yellow urine in the hourly measuring canister and collection bag.

'We will take the tube out in a day or two, when we can. This has been a really big day for you, Keith, so I will just get you washed before the men arrive to help me reposition you.'

At the thought of being moved, Keith looked stressed.

'I can give you more pain relief before we move you,' Chloe reassured him, softly patting her hand on top of his head. 'The main job for you overnight will be to report any pain or nausea, and to keep taking the deep breaths I showed you before, hourly when you are awake. We also need you to move your feet up and back to prevent clots. That is why those sequential compression device pumps are squeezing your legs'.

When Keith still looked anxious, Chloe reminded him that she will be present for the next seven hours overnight to keep him comfortable. Sheila embraced Chloe in a hug, saying, 'Thank you'. Before leaving, Sheila reminded Keith that she would be back at 10 am.

Chloe administered another 30 mcg of fentanyl intravenously for pain relief. Keith slept peacefully as Chloe gently washed him, removing the Betadine solution from his abdomen and groin. Chloe secured the indwelling catheter to Keith's leg to minimise any trauma caused by movement.

A few hours later, Chloe was startled by Keith defensively grabbing her arm as she lifted his blankets to check his surgical site for bleeding.

'Sorry, Chloe, I was having a silly dream.'

'Don't worry. Those narcotic painkillers can do that sometimes. Do you have any pain now?'

'Just a little.'

'On a scale of one to ten, with zero being no pain at all and 10 being really excruciating pain, how much would you rate your pain?'

'About two out of ten.'

'Okay, I will give you some more fentanyl now,' said Chloe in a soothing tone.

Keith woke up to a monitor beeping and Chloe's arm under his blankets replacing the lead that had disconnected.

'How is your pain now?'

'Gone, thanks, Chloe. Thank you for taking such good care of me.'

'You are most welcome. Your mum and dad rang about ten minutes ago, Keith. They said to send you their love.' Chloe bent to check his urine meter. 'Everything is going well. All your vital signs are stable. I have even started reducing the noradrenaline infusion supporting your blood pressure and the percentage of oxygen you are receiving.'

After more analgesia, Keith was stunned to find his mind had wandered to recalling Chloe's warm embrace in her white satin nightie, to the feel of her warm body beside his again. Keith slept again with dreams that had him reliving that cuddle. He awoke with an excruciating pain from the bladder tube as his body responded to his erotic thoughts.

Chapter 15

Chloe

Keith was automatically guarding his surgical wound each time I attempted to check the dressing for haemorrhage. When I moved his left hand to improve the tracing of Keith's arterial line displaying his blood pressure on the monitor screen, he held my hand, reluctant to let go. I needed to place Keith's wrist where the arterial line was inserted, into a position that would achieve the best waveform on the monitor, to get the most accurate reading. Periodically, Keith stared at me, possibly from the combined effects of his sepsis and the narcotics causing delirium. As his temperature peaked two degrees above normal, Keith gazed at me intensely, intermittently mumbling about a white satin lady. From what I could interpret from the rambling, he wanted to hug the lady he thought was embracing him.

'Did you let Keith's partner know he was in hospital?' I texted Sheila at eight the next morning, when I arrived home.

'What partner?'

'Keith's partner. Does she know he's in ICU? He kept talking about a lady he is very close to most of the night.'

'Oh? I'll come down,' responded Sheila.

I filled the kettle and switched it on just before Sheila knocked on the door.

'Keith's okay,' I reassured Sheila. 'He became febrile overnight to 39.1 degrees Celsius, so I collected some blood cultures. After his temperature spiked, the poor bugger had a terribly busy night ratting around in his bed.'

'What did he say?' questions Sheila smiling curiously.

'Not much really. His mumblings were about "white satin flowing" and how it "clung to her curves".'

Sheila buckles, laughing. 'Oh, *that* lady? Well, she is real, but she hardly knows poor Keith exists. And, yes, he is attracted to her. It's unrequited love, I'm afraid. Without invading Keith's privacy, I can't say too much. I'll just say that she's lovely but probably considers Keith more of a friend. They have never dated and aren't in a relationship.'

'Well, let me tell you that he desperately wanted to hold her last night. Don't you think you should at least let her know that he's in hospital? It could make a difference ...'

'Keith was probably just reliving an incident that happened between them,' Sheila explained

'An incident? I assumed the white satin was a wedding or debutante dress.'

'Well, the incident was an innocent mistake, really. I don't want you to tell Keith I told you this, but I'll try to explain broadly what happened, so you won't think he was too delirious. It started with a party. Keith was asleep in his bed and a lady accidentally climbed into the other side, not realising he was there. The next morning, Keith woke up, trapped. The lady was soundly asleep lying cuddled into him, with her head on his shoulder and her arm across his body. As a thorough gentleman, Keith had to lie there still, patiently waiting until she turned over again. The lady was in such a deep sleep, and he could not disentangle himself.'

'Oh, so she does not realise he is fond of her?'

'No, and you mustn't say anything either, please!'

'Oh. No, I won't. The way he spoke about the white satin I thought Keith was married.'

'No. Keith has been working at remote locations, living in roadside camps doing grading work. Keith is quite smitten with the lady, though. They would make such a lovely couple, too. Keith has a fairly quiet nature. He would never embarrass the lady by telling her what happened. Keith is more likely to just admire her from a distance, unless she was showing an interest in him. It's sad, really. Although Keith feels romantically attracted to her, he will never act on his feelings unless she indicated her attraction to him,' Sheila sighed.

'What a shame!'

Chapter 16

Keith

Although my appendectomy and bowel washout went well, after leaving the intensive care unit and being discharged from hospital to Sheila's, I continued to experience frequent bouts of abdominal pain. At 185 cm tall, my weight dropped to an alarming 55 kg. I could not eat as my brain kept associating food ingestion as a trigger for pain. When dining with my family, I continually pushed the food around on my plate, rather than putting it in my mouth, reluctant to trigger more colicky pain or diarrhoea.

On the occasions when I did eat, I would often be awake all night with a severe, unrelenting gut ache. At my six weeks' post-operative medical review in the surgical clinic, the alarmed surgeon told me I looked like skin and bone. I knew what he meant, since my chest was merely corrugated ribs with no fat, and my eye sockets and cheeks were hollow. I felt incredibly lethargic and was becoming fearful about dying.

'Tell me about your family history, Keith,' said Dr Strathdee. 'Is your mum and dad still alive? Are there any illnesses suffered by other family members?'

'Mum and Dad are fine. Dad is about 175 cm tall but he is only about 60 kgs, dripping wet, so he has always been thin.'

'But you were 73 kgs when you were first admitted, right? You are continuing to lose weight for some reason? Your blood tests show that your iron and calcium levels are becoming critically low. There is no hair on your arms and legs. This warrants further investigation.'

'Of my eight siblings, my dad, my youngest brother and three sisters have asthma. One of my younger sisters died of asthma and my brother has been admitted to intensive care with severe asthma. Two of my sisters also have eczema and skin allergies. Dad's side have allergies and mum's side have high cholesterol.'

'I think we will do a blood test. I suspect that your appendicitis was the symptom of a bigger problem, Keith. It is likely that bowel inflammation is causing the pain you describe when you try to eat. Yes, we will start with an anti-gliadin antibodies test to see if you're allergic to wheat. Then, we need to check your faeces for calprotectin to confirm whether bowel segments are inflamed, causing the pain triggered by eating. The laboratory tests and your weight loss are both indicating severe malabsorption. You have low iron and calcium levels because you are not absorbing nutrients from your bowel, as you should,' explained Dr Strathdee.

The doctor held his hands up, running his pointer finger around the side of his fingers on his other hand, saying, 'The finger-like protrusions called villi in your gut should be providing a large surface area for absorption, but it seems they may have flattened.'

He ran the same pointer finger along the knuckles of his closed fist, suggesting that my bowel's villi were flat like his knuckles rather than projecting like his fingers.

'Since you are getting loose bowel motions, I'd like both these tests done today. You cannot afford any further weight loss. I'd like to see you again on Friday when these labs are back. My nurse will book you in for the dietician Friday too. Hopefully by then, we will have a diagnosis to manage this weight loss.'

'Thanks, doc. I had expected after my appendix was removed that the belly ache would go away. I have been worrying about the pain recurring every time I eat.'

Disturbed by the blistering lesions on Keith's elbows that became visible as he stood up to leave, Dr Strathdee asked, 'Have you ever had these sores before this?'

'No,' said Keith, 'they are incredibly itchy and when I scratch them, they hurt. They are on my knees, too.'

Keith rolled up his trouser legs. Dr Strathdee moved closer, examining the sores with a light.

'Sorry, Keith, slight change of plans. I need to get a biopsy of these blisters as well before you go. My nurse will set up for the procedure, if you just wait outside the minor ops room. These blisters look very much like dermatitis herpetiformis.

The condition I was describing to you before is called coeliac disease. These blisters look like a variant of the coeliac disease called dermatitis herpetiformis, where you get both bowel inflammation and blisters from a wheat allergy. The biopsy of a blister that I get will need to be stained by the laboratory in a procedure called immunofluorescent studies. If I'm right, they will find wheat antibodies. These signs and symptoms often run in families and could also be responsible for the allergies you describe. Maybe even your dad's thinness.'

The excited doctor said, 'I usually only diagnose one of these cases a year.'

Chapter 17

Chloe

I drove into my unit's car park. As I left the car with my handbag and keys, I was surprised to see Keith Johnson in Sheila's car, sitting quietly, using the internet on his phone. My eyes widened in alarm, and I gasped involuntarily at his dramatic weight loss. Keith was looking pale and emaciated. He looked quite ill and had lost his usual vibrant appearance. How could he look worse than he had six weeks ago, when he was critically ill in ICU? Keith looked visibly upset and teary, I noticed as I moved closer.

'Hi, Keith.'

Looking distracted and sad, Keith glanced up from the device wearing a frown and looking worried. He tried to smile, but it failed to reach his eyes. The smile that emerged looked more like a grimace, almost as though he was acutely distressed. Keith nervously swallowed, as though something was terribly wrong, and dropped his head in his hands. I opened the passenger door and slid into the front seat beside him.

'Sorry, Chloe, I'm just having a rough day,' the miserable Keith explained. Using his hand, he began wiping away the tears spilling over.

'What's happened?' I asked passing him the small packet of tissues I'd retrieved from my handbag. In the silence, I reached over to put my arms on Keith's bony shoulders. He dropped his head again. His shoulders and head shook as he began sobbing uncontrollably.

'Sorry ... sorry ... I'm just hideous today ... I'm absolutely maxed! I have had enough of doctors and tests and being tired and getting pain when I eat ... I can't sleep for itching, and when I scratch, the doctor said I am ripping off my epidermis.' Keith leant forward, burying his reddening face in both his hands. 'I would tell you that I'm fed up, but I haven't been able to eat a bloody thing for about a week,' he sadly joked.

'Oh no! Show me these sores,' I replied, stunned.

Keith rotated his arms around and rolled up his trouser legs to show me the blistering sores respectively on his elbows and knees, and the biopsied site just lateral to his elbow flexure.

'I've just got no sense of humour left today! I'm sick of being sick and beyond frustrated,' Keith glumly replied. He leant forward, folding his hands over the steering wheel, resting his head on them to hide his face.

'So, you've seen a doctor today then?' I asked, trying to encourage him.

'Yes, and I go back again on Friday,' sighed Keith.

'What did he say?' I asked, curious to know more. 'You have lost a lot of weight, Keith. I hardly recognised you. You do look very ill.'

'I didn't really ever get over the gangrenous appendix. I haven't been able to eat or sleep much since,' the devastated Keith remarked. 'I was just looking up the words I wrote down. Dr Strathdee believes I have a malabsorption disorder. He said it is making parts of my bowel inflamed and stopping me from absorbing iron, calcium and nutrients. It's called this ...' showing me the word 'dermatitis herpetiformis' displayed on the screen.

'Well, that is good news, Keith! That condition is treated with a gluten-free diet. A gluten-free diet should make your pain, blisters and itching stop. The diet will stop the inflammation in your bowel, so you can absorb nutrients and put on weight again.'

Intrigued by my upbeat response, Keith uncovered his face to look up at me in dismay. He was wondering if I was serious.

'You think so?' he questioned ambivalently. Keith's eyebrows rose optimistically, as though he was grasping for any shred of positivity.

'Come with me in my car', I said. 'You're not well, so let me kidnap you for the afternoon.'

I sprang out of Keith's car, leading him by his hand to my vehicle.

I am going to take you to my favourite place and then we will go shopping for gluten-free food,' I say, excitedly, challenging Keith with the prospect of an adventure.

I took Keith to a small specialty food shop that sold vegan, diabetic and gluten-free food. I enthusiastically scooped gluten-free Jaffas and other snacks into separate plastic bags.

'You will love these, they are delicious.'

Next, I eagerly pointed to all the foods in the tubs that were gluten-free, showing Keith the wheat-free symbol. Carrying a basket loaded up with gluten-free health bars, fruit and nut slices, rice and almond crunches, jubes and biscuits, I stopped at the gelato bar.

'We will start you with soft gluten-free foods first. What flavour gelato would you like'?

'Coffee?' Keith indicated his uncertainty that he would keep anything down.

'Pick another. We'll get two different scoops each and taste each other's flavours. I'll buy two extra spoons.'

Not looking at all confident that he would be able to eat the gelatos without pain, Keith hesitantly pointed to the mango flavour.

'Okay, we need four gluten-free scoops, please,' I advised the shop assistant. 'The scoops of coffee and mango will be for one cup, and the other cup will be strawberry and vanilla, thanks.'

Sitting in my car like schoolkids, Keith and I sample each other's gelato flavours. The malnourished Keith is surprised to experience no pain.

Building on my success, I took Keith to the supermarket to buy more gluten-free products. Starting him on a soft light diet, I bought gluten-free custard, a tub of choc chip, chocolate and vanilla ice cream, barramundi, gravies, biscuits, snacks and high protein milk drinks.

'If we restrict your diet to soft gluten-free foods in small portions of about five to seven meals a day, you should stay pain free and begin to absorb nutrients again. With no wheat going in, the bowel inflammation and pain should go. Since you like fish, we will start with pan-fried barramundi for dinner. I'll cook it. Oh, we will need to find gluten-free tartare sauce. Will Sheila be home?'

'No, Sheila's gone home to Mum and Dad's. She might be back later, but not for dinner. I haven't told them any of this news yet. I am waiting until Friday to have the diagnosis confirmed. I am still trying to wrap my head around all this myself,' Keith confessed. 'Sheila will stay home and have tea there with our parents, I expect.'

'All this food is edible, Keith, so it does not matter whether you need gluten-free or not. If we try soft, small gluten-free meals, and there is less pain, it will be a win,' I add cheekily, 'especially if I am cooking.'

'Deal!' said Keith, carrying some of our grocery bags into Sheila's unit.

'Tonight, we will skip the vegies that are high in fibre to avoid stirring up your tummy. We are just going to try to get you to keep some mashed pumpkin, mashed potatoes and a small fish serve and sauce down.'

'Okay. I never really feel hungry these days, but I will try.'

I cooked the pan-fried barramundi to perfection. Even

though Keith had enjoyed the meal, he seemed to love my company more.

'How about a movie?' Keith suggested, not wanting our pleasant evening to end. 'You pick. Sheila has loads of romantic comedies and chick flicks here. If you like Sandra Bullock, there's *Two Weeks Notice*.'

'Mmm, I do'.

'Or Sheila's got lots of BBC classics like *Pride and Prejudice*, *North and South* ...'

'*Two Weeks Notice* sounds good to me, if you like it? I like good comedy.'

'Deal. I'll get some juices.'

'Can I suggest you dilute yours? Just fill the glass to a quarter with juice then top the glass up with water, while your tummy is more sensitive. That way, you should not run into problems with too much acid.'

'Do you feel like apple, orange or orange and passionfruit juice?'

'Oooh, I do love orange and passionfruit.'

Keith arrived with the juices, saying in a flirty tone, 'Well, Miss Chloe, your mission is accomplished. I have had a small protein meal with no pain or diarrhoea yet.'

'Yahoo!' I said with a fist pump. 'We'll get there!'

'Yes, we can't let all your excellent ICU nursing care go to waste.'

'Definitely not! You've had a more turbulent recovery than was anticipated, though.'

'Once I was out of ICU, off all those antibiotics and drips

and out of hospital, I had expected to be fine. I was shocked when Dr Strathdee said today he thought the gangrenous appendicitis seemed to have been just a symptom of a bigger issue. I was shaken when he said that, in my case with the ongoing weight loss and malabsorption, the cause still needed to be addressed.'

'Well, tonight has given us more hope that soft gluten-free, small meals might work.'

'I am truly grateful for all your help,' Keith said sincerely, maintaining eye contact. 'I was in such a sorry state this afternoon. It feels like I have no energy and that everything is so difficult. Everything seems to be requiring more stamina than I possess at the moment. I didn't come here to be a burden to Sheila, after the ordeal she has been going through.'

'Well, you've no confirmation of the diagnosis yet, but I believe Dr Strathdee is on the right track, from what you've said after tonight's meal. And as you saw, it wasn't that hard to find the gluten-free food, was it? Once you knew to look for the symbol with the wheat in a circle and the strike through it, it made our mission of finding the food in the deli, much easier, didn't it? Whatever the diagnosis is, know that we can all help you. I'm confident of that'.

I leant across, lightly patting Keith's left hand. Keith responded by gently folding his fingers over my hand.

'When you are as sick as you have been and with malabsorption issues on top, you tend to find your energy wanes easily, especially with low iron levels.'

'Yes, I've been in despair, worrying about finding the

energy to be able to work again.'

'That may take some time. Once the bowel inflammation stops, the malabsorption should correct slowly. You should start putting on weight again. I don't want to frighten you, Keith, but, while I think of it, can I also remind you that any tablets, medicines and cough mixtures will need to be gluten-free too. I have been told by patients the main challenge with the gluten-free foods is finding the sauces, soups, yoghurts, gravies and breads you like. There are often so many numbers and additives, that most coeliac people tell me they rely on the labelling and symbol. Tomorrow, I have another day off so let's have another shopping adventure for gluten-free sausages and rissoles that don't have any wheat cereal binders. We can get some gluten-free cereals, breads and bread rolls too. Most patients say the breads tend to be heavier. They always ask us to toast the breads.'

'Tomorrow sounds great. Thank you for helping me. I truly appreciate it. If I can ever get through all this, Chloe, would you come out to dinner with me? I like being with you. I don't just mean as a one off; I mean I would like to date you ... long-term.'

'I am sorry, Keith. I wouldn't feel right about that, not when I know that you are very attracted to another lady. All night when you were in ICU, you talked about her.'

Frowning, Keith looked puzzled, gazing at me intently.

'I don't know what I might have said, when you had my brain pickled with painkillers. All I can tell you is that I want to be your boyfriend. I want to feel you hugging me again.'

'Keith, sometimes when you get as sick as you have been, especially with malabsorption issues, your brain does not get enough carbohydrates. The brain is carbohydrate dependent, so it can play tricks on you and affect your comprehension. I hadn't ever hugged you until you were upset in your car today. I didn't hug you before you went into the ICU.'

Keith dropped his head. 'I'm making a muck of this, aren't I? I can only tell you truly, Chloe, that there is no one else. I want to be with you, and not just for your nursing skills. I liked you before that, as a person.'

'I think your brain has made you forget her, because you have been so ill.'

'Chloe, from the moment I met you, I only wanted to date you. Please believe me, all that night in the ICU, I was thinking only about you,' he says pointing at her.

'No, Keith. You're confused. You called her "the lady in the white satin", the one who hugged you.'

'That ... that was *you*!'

'No, no, you're just confused, Keith. I had never hugged you before today.'

Keith dropped his head silently, not wanting to argue.

'What made you think it was me?' I was confused by this turn of our conversation.

'I know it was you ... but I don't want to upset you.'

'What do you mean, "upset me"? Are you saying I was sleepwalking?'

'No. Sheila had asked us all for space after Brett died. I was working too far out of town for weekend visits then. I wanted to catch up with Sheila, and when I began getting the stomach pains, I came over to Sheila's on a Friday night to ask her opinion about them. I woke in the morning, and you were in the bed with me. You had me pinned down.'

'What!'

I was convinced that Keith was fatiguing from his iron deficiency and accumulative health issues.

'I'm sorry I didn't tell you. I didn't want to embarrass you. I promise nothing untoward happened. I tried to get Sheila to lift your arm, to help me get up. Sheila saw me pinned down and laughed. It was the first time she had laughed naturally in ages ... since Brett died, really, I suppose. Sheila, as you know, was still grieving. Suddenly she brightened into her usual teasing self, using my predicament as an opportunity to wind me up. She snapped some pictures with her phone and pretended to be sending them to Mum and Dad. Don't worry, she didn't send them any pictures, of course. I loved seeing Sheila jovial again that day. I'm sorry, Chloe, but the girl in the white satin was you in your nightie. You had a green, apricot and white brunch coat that you wore with it. The brunch coat was draped over the end of the bed.'

'I don't think it was me. I have no recollection.' I was bewildered.

'Yes, it was you. Sheila was in a teasing mood, sending me the pics on my phone all day. It was the first time Sheila was back to her usual prankster self. You looked so cute ... I kind of saved every one of them.'

Keith looked guilty and ashamed of his conduct. I was

now more confused than ever.

'I don't want you to think that we were being disrespectful or invading your privacy,' Keith added defensively.

'Show me,' I demanded, withdrawing my hand and feeling worried.

'You were dressed ... I'm sorry,' said Keith, anxious and panicked at upsetting me.

Keith dropped his face into his hands, sitting still and stunned, exhibiting visible signs of emotional distress. He looked too sick to decide what to do for the best and angry at himself for ruining the lovely evening we had been enjoying together.

'Keith, it's okay. You are just mixing me up with someone else,' I patiently persisted. I moved closer, wrapping my arms around the distraught Keith's shoulders to calm him, but it seemed it was my proximity that soothed him rather than any spoken word.

'Will you ... will you please come out with me? I know what I want, and it is only you, Chloe. There is no mistake. I like your personality, your kindness, your wit, your looks, your gentle nature ... everything about you.'

'You go get your phone, Keith, and I will try to see if I can help you figure out who it is,' I said in a soothing tone.

Reluctant to upset me, Keith sat frozen, immobilised by fear. Keith seemed acutely aware that I had not answered his question. Keith seemed not to want to frighten me away, especially when this was the most time we had ever spent together, the closest we had ever been. Keith sat quietly, his head dropped and both hands covering his face, visibly distraught.

'All right then, Keith, we will just watch the movie for now,' I said, diverting him from stress he had no energy for.

I sat patiently beside the distraught Keith, keeping my arm around his bony shoulders, relieved by his now passively still body language. Warmed by my body and fatigued from his long day, Keith began dozing off. Concerned about Keith's agitation and vulnerability, my thoughts were on overload. Yes, I realised I had always liked the handsome olive-skinned Keith, although my interaction with him so far had been limited. I had enjoyed holding his hands and caring for him in ICU. I liked his gentle touch. I could not deny that I felt some attraction to him. However, I was not one to take advantage of his frailty.

As the movie finished, I went upstairs to grab a pillow and blanket. I lay Keith's head down on the lounge, placing a pillow underneath his head and a blanket on top before quietly shutting the door behind me.

I had witnessed Keith freeze with uncertainty when I had asked to see the photos, as if my request was a huge risk. Becoming neurotic, I had even checked my pyjamas and nighties, looking for anything that looked remotely white satin but found nothing.

All night, I tossed and turned, recalling the strong physical attraction drawing me towards Keith, when he had held my hand in the ICU. It was only with reluctance and out of respect for the other lady that I had detached my hand when

Keith had settled. I had looked in his chart for his partner's contact number. I felt hideously conflicted. On the one hand, I longed for more of Keith's charming smile, gentle hugs and touch, but I was also desperate not to be heartbroken or rejected when the other lady showed up.

The brief physical contact I had enjoyed with Keith had brought on a loneliness I had not experienced since Dad had died. I was also hesitant to be bonding to a vulnerable male who was the brother of my dear friend. My feelings of longing to see Keith again made the dilemma more unsettling. Emotionally, I did not feel strong enough to cope with further loss in my life, after the death of my parents, the sale of our home and the recent reduced contact with my siblings.

Chapter 18

Chloe

I had removed my hand from Keith's when he told me about the white satin lady, because I couldn't bear to be hurt. I was afraid of being attracted to him. I yearned for more of his gentle touch, charming smiles and warm conversations. I had enjoyed the afternoon we had just spent together. Life was hard enough being an orphan, with my siblings and I traumatised from childhood abuse, without setting myself up for further emotional pain.

I needed to protect myself from the risk of having a partner, mistaking his affection for me, with his feelings for someone else. My emotions were in turmoil. Worse still my body was betraying me, with feelings of desire for Keith. I was craving more of his touch. Each time Keith had held my hand, I found myself enjoying his contact and seeking more of his tenderness.

When Keith had bravely asked me last night to date him, I did not believe such an opportunity could be conceivable. My brain warned me that we were too different to be compatible. Keith and I were polar opposites. While Keith has a large, normal, loving family who valued him, I grew up victimised and treated as worthless. I existed in a hostile environment with fear and aggression, experiencing daily the worst of humanity. My Irate Irene experiences taught me to hate and mistrust humanity, since the strong always seemed to oppress and destroy the vulnerable. Rather than being destructive, Keith's kind large family loved each other, in an inclusive, constructive way. His normal environment was so alien to mine it was terrifying.

With my month of holidays having just begun, I decided to spend the day with Keith at the beach after his doctor's appointment. I was hoping that packing up for a picnic and a swim might blunt the impact of his diagnosis.

Before I went to collect Keith, I texted him to say that I was blending up a yoghurt, banana and berries gluten-free smoothie to share for our breakfast. Blending and juicing tend to be the one of the fastest ways to restore nutrients, in a more absorbable liquid form. I told Keith that I was kidnapping him for another day of fun and adventure, hoping I could help him to transition into the gluten-free lifestyle with less turbulence.

I was selfishly aware of wanting to spend the day together, because I was seeking more of his company and contact. Now that I had made the scary decision to let my heart lead, I also made a General Practitioner appointment for tomorrow to obtain a contraceptive script. I found myself actually experiencing envy when I thought of the white satin lady embracing Keith in his bed. I wanted to be the one holding him captive in my embrace. How could I be missing him already when I only left him ten hours ago? I was becoming addicted to this quiet, handsome man with his tender manners. Keith's asking me to date long-term gave me more confidence to plan to spend more of my holidays with him.

At 10.45 am, I attended Keith's appointment with Dr Strathdee to provide support and to use my nursing knowledge to help Keith navigate the lifestyle changes ahead. The skin biopsy confirmed that Keith was indeed suffering from dermatitis herpetiformis. Although I had seen the blisters clustered on Keith's knees and elbows, Dr Strathdee's examination had confirmed that the symmetrical, excoriated, blistering and crusted lesions were also on Keith's occipital ridge of his scalp, his sacrum, buttocks and his scapula in the classical pattern. With the exception of one larger blister on Keith's left elbow, most of the vesicles were 3 mm to 5 mm in diameter.

Where the blistering rash had healed, evidence of the inflammatory skin damage remained visible as hypo- and hyper-pigmented areas. The doctor informed Keith that the 100 mg of dapsone he was prescribing would stop the wheat antibody blisters erupting from his skin, causing the persistent itching. When he did scratch, cavities were left, leaving painful ulcers as Keith was inevitably removing his top layer of epidermis. Dr Strathdee instructed Keith to bathe in a lightly tinted pink bath of Condy's crystals to stop the itching. The doctor had also documented Keith's brittle scalp hair and the loss of lateral eyebrows as signs of malnutrition or possible thyroid gland antibody issues.

Although Keith had remained blissfully unaware that his new diagnosis would affect his ability to work at the remote campsites where he had previously been employed, I was hoping that the prospect of a new relationship might lessen the impact. In his fragile state, Keith's extended sick leave and the mandatory lifestyle adjustments needed to be taken a day at a time. He needed access to fresh fruit and vegetables for blending and juicing, along with five to seven meals a day, to help his weight loss recovery.

Dr Strathdee informed Keith that his dermatitis herpetiformis was much more than just a wheat allergy with blisters. It was an autoimmune skin disease that also affected his bowel integrity. While the dapsone would stop the blisters occurring, he would require frequent blood tests for the side effects of this medication until the dapsone could be eventually tapered off. The gluten-free diet would be required lifelong to prevent bowel inflammation and pain. In holding Keith's hand, I encouraged him to interpret this new knowledge in a positive light. The gluten-free diet would allow Keith to be able to eat without fearing the pain, nausea and diarrhoea he associated with food.

Dr Strathdee informed Keith that his skin and the associated bowel disorder were most likely genetic in origin.

The doctor explained dermatitis herpetiformis was caused by deposits of immunoglobulin A in the skin, and that those deposits triggered immune reactions with his skin antigens in a cycle that would be interrupted with the dapsone.

'Did having my appendix out cause all this?' Keith asked, confused. His fatigued expression warned Dr Strathdee that Keith's attention was already overwhelmed.

'Appendicitis can be caused by bowel inflammation, Keith, but the most likely factor triggering your condition was your age and possessing a genetic tendency.'

Dr Strathdee reassured Keith that dermatitis herpetiformis often initially presents in males between the ages of twenty-eight and thirty years, more commonly in Caucasians. Using the internet, Dr Strathdee informed Keith that the incidence of his condition was one in ten thousand of the population.

I also reported my concern to the doctor about Keith's comprehension being impaired by his weight loss and prolonged illness. I described how Keith had deposited a cheque into his bank account and was distressed when the balance available had not changed. At the time, despite my explanation, Keith had been unable to comprehend the difference between the balance on the bank teller's receipt and amount available, when cheques required several days to clear. To evaluate Keith's comprehension, Dr Strathdee instructed him to respond to a serious of random comments in any way that he felt was appropriate.

For example, Dr Strathdee suggested, 'The last carriage of a train is always involved in an accident. I think we should remove the last carriage.'

'That would be a good idea,' Keith responded seriously to the absurd statement.

In failing the comprehension test that the doctor had used for his assessment, it was apparent that Keith would need more sick leave. He should also not drive or operate machinery until his health improved.

The good news for Keith was that the incessant itching and sleeplessness that had resulted from the skin deposits would begin subsiding within one hour after taking 100 mg of dapsone. Dr Strathdee advised Keith that his itching would continue to dissipate within forty-eight to seventy-two hours, with no new blisters appearing after twenty-four to thirty-six hours. We therefore changed our beach plans to maximise this itching relief, using the time for Keith to have a Condy's crystals bath before he saw the dietician.

The first stop after the hospital outpatient appointment was to get the dapsone and Condy's crystals at the chemist. Knowing Sheila was at work, we tinted Keith's bathwater with only a few of the tiny crystals to get the light pink solution required to achieve the antimicrobial effects and remove the scabs forming from the excoriated blisters. Keith and I both sat in the light pink solution in our togs, knowing that we had to return to the hospital within two hours for his dietician review. Recalling Keith's distress on the previous Wednesday, I hoped that spending the day together might buffer Keith from the lifestyle changes being thrust upon him. In order to buffer the impact of so many changes occurring simultaneously, and with Keith's comprehension levels fluctuating, we decided to keep our growing relationship a secret for the time being.

However, the bad news was that the dapsone might need to be continued for one to two years to prevent the raised, red, papular skin bumps and vesicles from re-forming. The formation of the blisters and ongoing gut pain had been a shock and disappointment to Keith, who had been expecting a full recovery after his appendix removal. After two months of weight loss, endless itching and sleep deprivation, I was encouraging Keith to be excited that his new diagnosis had a treatment. I was now hoping that I could spend my holidays learning what Keith's favourite foods were to make this transition smoother.

At 2 pm, I attended Keith's dietician review with him to support his dietary changes and ease his escalating concerns about his diminished memory, concentration and comprehension. The dietician, Judy, educated Keith that his dermatitis herpetiformis condition was caused by his sensitivity to the gliadin fraction of the protein in wheat, rye and barley called 'gluten'. Judy re-enforced that eating foods with gluten would trigger the intense, burning immune reaction in his skin and also precipitate weight loss, gut pain and bloating.

'Oh God,' gasped Keith, rubbing his face suddenly in frustration. 'I just remembered that I had increased my lunch to six slices of bread after my appendectomy, trying to stop the weight loss. My clothes were getting baggy. I had to buy a belt to keep my trousers from falling down. No wonder the pain got worse!'

'Yes, that probably didn't help, Keith, but you weren't to know. But now the important thing to remember is that you don't need to go without any of your favourite foods. My role is to teach you to replace the foods you like, with gluten-free brands that you can tolerate.'

Judy provided a food list. Keith was told to expect that that the IgA antibodies deposited in his skin would continue to flare up for weeks to months, causing the digestive symptoms of his gluten intolerance. Judy highlighted that although the name dermatitis herpetiformis was derived from medical terms that described blisters forming in clusters that resembled Herpes, his condition was not caused by any virus or sexually transmitted disease.

On Keith's next weekly visit to Dr Strathdee, he was instructed to use lubricating eye drops, sprays and sun-tinted glasses to relieve his new dry eye problem. The doctor told Keith that his dry and irritated eyes were just another symptom associated with his condition, as he was not producing sufficient tears to keep his eyes moist. Dr Strathdee advised Keith that his dry eyes could also be a sign of vitamin A deficiency, given his malabsorption problems. Keith had a thyroid function test added to his usual liver function tests, vitamin B12, iron and folic acid studies, calcium and full blood count. Keith's haemoglobin had remained at 100 gm/L due to his poor iron uptake and the gluten-sensitive bowel enteropathy causing the flattened villi (the finger-like structures of the intestinal lining) reducing the absorption area for nutrients.

Dr Strathdee again re-enforced that although the dapsone would reduce the visible skin lesions, the gluten-free diet had to be adhered to for the rest of his life. Dr Strathdee reiterated that with dermatitis herpetiformis autoimmune disorder, absolute compliance was crucial, as for the first five years after diagnosis, patients had a significant six to ten times greater risk of getting a cancer called non-Hodgkin lymphoma. Ingesting a gluten-free diet was also beneficial in enhancing nutrient absorption, maintaining bone density and reducing the risk of developing other autoimmune conditions. So far, adherence to the gluten-free diet had not been an issue. Even when Keith smelled delicious foods that stimulated his appetite, we had been able to find a gluten-free substitute.

The doctor was delighted to find that Keith's weight had increased by two kilograms since his last visit. Keith visibly threw his head back in disbelief, when the surgeon predicted that it would take at least two years for his intestinal villi to return to their normal finger-like shape and function, and to achieve his normal minimum weight of 72 kg.

Although Keith was feeling less pain and brain fog on the gluten-free diet and benefiting from an improved sleep, his fatigue from his iron deficiency anaemia worsened when the dapsone caused his red cells to break up prematurely, a side effect called haemolysis. Keith became short of breath and more fatigued after his low haemoglobin plummeted further to 80 gms/L. To combat Keith's falling red cell count, Dr

Strathdee reduced the dapsone down to 50mg daily, then to 50mg every second day, as his skin remained intact.

Dr Strathdee was also amazingly supportive and thorough in keeping Keith's supervisor informed of his diagnosis, progress and ongoing complications. However, when Keith's condition had improved sufficiently to permit a graduated return to work, he resigned within a week. Keith felt too weak physically to challenge the ignorant comments of colleagues attributing his rapid weight loss to the AIDS virus. The final straw which led Keith to abruptly vote with his feet was loud verbal abuse while he was attempting to eat his lunch.

'Fancy breads won't cure the clap, mate,' a road worker vocalised, utterly humiliating Keith. 'You're not fooling anybody here,' he continued in an ignorant slur. 'I saw that rash in the war.'

While Keith was visibly upset as he packed up his belongings to drive back permanently to his room in Sheila's unit, he was unprepared for the dramas yet to come.

Chapter 19

The Johnson family

Fatigued from his drive, Keith apologised to Sheila about his early return. Unwilling to relive the recent trauma he had been subjected to, Keith went to his room for a rest, leaving Sheila concerned but light on details. Sheila was aware that Keith had been sleeping poorly, as he had begun closing his bedroom more often to reduce noises. Before he had left, Keith and Chloe had been eating most of their meals together, since Sheila was working, sleeping or visiting their parents. On his arrival, Keith had texted Chloe, asking her to take the verandah route to his room. After the demoralising day he had endured, Keith was keen to experience more of the comforting cuddles he had missed all week.

Before Keith and Chloe could inform Sheila or Keith's parents of his new diagnosis and lifestyle changes, his parents arrived, hammering at the unit door. Sheila was gobsmacked not only to find her mum and dad in her doorway, but both unintelligibly sobbing, talking about dying and terminal illnesses.

'Are you both okay?' Sheila asked, wondering which of her parents was ill.

'Why didn't you tell us he was dying?' sobbed grief-stricken Lizzy accusingly.

'Who's dying, Mum?'

'Keith! Why didn't you tell us how sick he was?'

'Well, he was all right a minute ago,' replied Sheila, looking towards the stairs. 'He's just gone upstairs for a rest. You know Keith is still getting over his gangrenous appendix and surgery. I was here when Keith said he would come and see you, when he was feeling a bit better.'

'Barney just rang from Kilkivan and told us he's dying!' confronts Lionel.

'Well, you know what Barney's like. He's not the sharpest tool in the shed!'

'So, Keith's okay?'

'Of course he is. Why wouldn't he be?'

'He's lost a lot of weight.'

'Yes, Dr Strathdee is looking after him. I told you that,' Sheila calmly reminded them, puzzled at her parent's distress. 'Keith sees the surgeon every week.'

'Did Keith have a blood transfusion?' asked Lizzy.

'Not that I am aware of, Mum. Chloe just said that Keith had noradrenaline and antibiotics for his septic shock.'

116

'But Keith resigned today. Barney's friends at Kilkivan said he's come home to die.'

'Die from what?' Sheila questioned frowning.

'AIDS, they told us! Keith got AIDS!' Lizzy said, bursting into tears. 'That's why he has lost so much weight.'

'That's nonsense, Mum! Utter garbage! Besides, Dr Strathdee is a surgeon, not an infection control consultant! How about we both come over on the weekend?'

'No, Sheila. Stop hiding him. I want to see my boy now!' Lionel demanded, raising his voice.

'Mum, Dad, seriously! You know he has been sick. Keith has just driven back from Kilkivan. He's exhausted and I am not going to wake him up because Barney is spouting his usual nonsense,' insisted Sheila. 'Keep your voice down, Dad, or Keith will be grumpy if you wake him up.'

Spinning on his heels, Lionel bolted up the stairs to Keith's bedroom, taking the steps two at a time, determined to resolve the matter. Without knocking, Lionel barged in. He was shocked to find both Chloe and Keith lying fully dressed on the bed. Lizzy, who had followed Lionel's rapid ascent up the stairs, had to abruptly change direction when he suddenly baulked rather than entering the room. Keith, who was sleeping soundly, spooning Chloe, woke up with a fright as the door burst open.

'Mum! Dad! What are you doing here?'

'Are you all right, son?' asked Lionel, anxiously scanning the hollowed cheeks and eye sockets of Keith's face.

'I'm making progress, Dad. Dr Strathdee said it will take

two years for a full recovery.'

'What does?' questioned Sheila, entering the room.

Sheila was unashamedly delighted at seeing the blushing Chloe so close to her brother.

'It's getting crowded in here,' said Lizzy. 'Come down for a cuppa and you can update us all, on what is going on.'

'Yes, we all need an update,' smirked Sheila, winking at Chloe.

Firmly holding the blushing Chloe's hand, Keith moved off the bed, following his family downstairs. Keith was very aware that it was going to be awkward enough for the orphaned Chloe to meet his large family, without his parents having found them lying together on a bed.

On the way down, Keith whispered to Chloe, 'Don't worry, it's okay. They know we are adults.'

The speechless, beetroot-red Chloe just nodded and tightened her grip. Sheila laughed, teasing her brother by using their usual levity to break the tension. At the bottom of the stairs, to de-escalate the tension, Sheila gave Chloe a hug. Smiling widely, she announced, 'This is the lovely Chloe, my good friend – and Keith's bedmate, apparently! That sight was even better than the pictures...' When Keith's jaw tightened with stress, Sheila added, 'This is our mum, Lizzy, and our dad, Lionel.' Both Lizzy and Lionel moved forward to hug the shell-shocked Chloe.

Seeing Lizzy unable to take her eyes off her gaunt son, Keith's head dropped suddenly and tears dripped down his gaunt face.

'I can't explain any of this, Mum. I can't even remember any of the names of what I've got yet!' Keith exclaimed, grabbing tissues to mop his sodden face. Keith's husky voice and shattered expression triggered tears in Chloe's eyes. She instantly embraced Keith, leaving the room silent.

'Well, I can try my best if you like, Keith,' Chloe offered, making eye contact with him. 'I know you wanted more time to tell them yourself, but your parents both look really worried.'

'Yes, you tell them, Chloe. It has all been needles and pain to me. I can't remember most of what's been said. I just know I can't take any more,' Keith tearfully pleaded, hugging Chloe closer. Sitting together, with her arm around Keith's waist, she took a deep breath.

'Okay,' began Chloe. 'Keith kept losing weight and his abdominal pain did not go away after his surgery. He started having six slices of bread for lunch, but his pain got worse. Blisters and crusted sores started appearing on his elbows and knees. Keith could not sleep because of the itching, and when he scratched, ulcers appeared because he was accidentally scratching off his top layer of skin.'

Chloe looked at Sheila for support as she continued.

'Keith's weight dropped to 55 kg because eating was causing him pain. Dr Strathdee biopsied the blisters and the laboratory dyed them, which is a test called immunofluorescent studies. The tests showed that Keith has an allergy to wheat, a genetic condition called dermatitis herpetiformis. To stop the blisters coming out, Keith has to take a drug called dapsone which needs weekly blood tests. Keith needs to have a gluten-free diet for life, because the bowel structures called villi have all flattened, reducing his surface area to absorb nutrients, causing malabsorption problems, particularly low calcium and iron levels. Unfortunately, a side effect of the dapsone has caused Keith's haemoglobin or red cell count to drop to 80, so he has been battling anaemia and shortness of breath too.'

'Oh, honey, you poor boy,' said Lizzy soothingly, hugging her tearful son. 'Why didn't you tell us?'

'I just feel tired the entire time, Mum. I couldn't remember the name of this condition, the name of the drugs ... anything.'

'Part of the problem with the flattened villi in his bowel and his severe weight loss is that the malnutrition and malabsorption have been affecting his comprehension, concentration and memory functions. Keith sometimes gets confused and a bit overwhelmed with everything because he's not been absorbing nutrients,' elaborated Chloe.

'I still can't say the blood name of it, Dad,' Keith said, shaking his head.

'Then with Keith still anaemic from the surgery, his haemoglobin dropped further and he started getting short of breath. In addition to the iron deficiency, the anaemia was also a side effect of the dapsone, which can prematurely smash up his red cells,' Chloe concluded.

'Barney rang me today, saying that you were dying,' explained Lionel. 'That bloody idiot had us so panicked we nearly had an accident racing over here.'

'Well, Keith's blisters, belly aches and diarrhoea have

all stopped. He thinks he's clever now after putting on five kilograms,' Chloe cheerfully adds to lighten the mood.

Sheila wandered around the table to hug Chloe.

'You have been the best friend ever, helping Keith through all this. I'm still missing Brett terribly, and probably too absorbed in my own misery still,' Sheila apologetically said.

'We managed fine, didn't we, Keith?' Chloe said, 'It might be worth you all coming on Friday, though. So far, Dr Strathdee has been trying to get Keith stable. If you could all spare two hours, you should ask to have the antigliadin tests done too, since this is an inherited condition.' Checking her phone diary Chloe added, 'Yes, it will be two hours. Keith sees Dr Strathdee at 1.15 pm then he usually has his bloods done after that. We could wait in the canteen to see Judy, the dietician. That appointment is for 2.30 pm. Oh, and I have some brochures and information on food brands to buy,' said Chloe, jogging up the stairs to get them.

'Are you two together?' asked Sheila and Lizzy in unison, once Chloe is out of sight.

'I hope so.' Keith smiled at their keenness.

'She's a keeper, son', whispered Lionel, placing a supportive hand on Keith's bony shoulder.

'I hope you won't be upset, but I resigned today, Dad,' Keith cautiously mentioned.

'How can I be upset when you're getting better and have put on 5 kgs?'

'And going to live!' added his mother.

'Chloe and I have had a talk. When I'm better, I'd like to

go to TAFE and learn to be a mechanic. I'd like to be able to fix the machines as well as drive them,' Keith added, smiling cheerfully. 'I don't think it will be two years before I can start my courses, though. My comprehension is getting better. It's just the anaemia making me feel washed out now.'

Chloe returned with some pamphlets and the gluten-free biscuits she had retrieved from Keith's room. Chloe left again to retrieve the box of gluten-free gravies, biscuits, orange Jaffas, jubes and snacks she had not yet unpacked from her car.

'We haven't really used any of the pure cornflour, or gluten-free plain and self-raising flour yet. We tried the gluten-free frozen crepes and Keith liked them with savoury mince, seafood and chicken, with avocado fillers.'

Checking her groceries list, Chloe added, 'Oh, that's right. I should mention too, that we found an article recommending plastic, not paper, straws. Apparently, the glue for the paper straws is made with flour and water – we hadn't thought about that. According to this little book, thickeners to be avoided have the numbers assigned to them between 1400 and 1450, mainly modified cornflour, starch, maltodextrin and dextrin. We found Keith some gluten-free pies, sausage rolls, breads and slices in the grocery shops.'

'Anyway,' Keith said cheekily, 'the main thing I can tell you for sure is that this is all your fault. Yes, Sheila,' Keith said, pointing to his parents, 'Dr Strathdee says they gave us the shallow end of the gene pool.'

Sheila laughed, relieved to see Keith being his usual cheeky self.

Looking at his sister, Keith continued to banter. 'I might not be able to say the name of this condition, or spell it, but I do remember that my main disability was called S-h-e-i-l-a.'

'My goodness, what a difference ten minutes makes,' remarked Chloe. 'Everyone has gone from crying to laughing.'

'Well, I am having the best day I have had in a while,' taunted Sheila. 'I wish I had not been behind Mum and Dad when they burst into your room. The looks on their faces would have been priceless.'

'I'm not really sure who got the biggest shock,' laughed Keith, shrugging with his arms upturned towards each of his parents.

'If you had told me a half an hour ago that we would go from death row to welcoming a new family member, I would not have managed the leap,' smirked Lionel.

'I had no idea that Chloe was in there. I was trying to convince them to let you sleep,' claimed Sheila innocently.

'We really needed to see for ourselves that you were okay,' rationalised Lizzy. 'Bloody Barney and his idle gossip! Neither one of us could have left without seeing you. He had us convinced you were dying. Barney said that Keith must have been given contaminated blood. We are sorry for busting in on you like that. Our imaginations got the better of us.'

'Oh,' gasped Chloe, too nervous to be following the conversation as well as she should have been. 'What did you think we were doing?'

Caught off guard, Sheila laughed until she coughed, spraying soft drink everywhere.

'I thought my son was dying, not bonking,' Lizzy clarified.

Sheila leant forward, swallowing the peanuts she'd been crunching to get Chloe's attention.

'So, are you two an item, then?'

'No ...' said Chloe, looking uncertainly at Keith, unsure what to say. 'Keith is smitten with the white satin lady. We talked about that, remember? I'd never take advantage of Keith while his comprehension is affected. Surely you know that.'

Sheila folded over, erupting with hilarity again, while Keith flushed and dropped his head in shame. Lizzy and Lionel looked from Sheila to Keith, bewildered.

'I'm going to let you dig me out of that awkward predicament, sis, since you created it.'

'What mischief have you been up to this time, Sheila?' Lionel smiled, pointing his finger at his mischievous daughter.

'Nothing, Dad,' said Sheila, wide-eyed and innocent. 'Keith had gone to bed one Friday night soon after he got here, after working all day. I forgot to tell Chloe he was coming. Chloe has a key to the upstairs bedroom, so she can walk along from her unit to get some sleep when Gabby and her friends party too much. Chloe must have come through the door on that side and slid into bed in the dark, not realising it was occupied. All I did was come out of my room. I looked up when I heard a hiss. My best friend Chloe was sound asleep, draped over Keith.'

'What!' Chloe looked stunned.

Keith looked worried, squeezing her hand for reassurance.

He had liked hearing Chloe talking about 'us' and 'we', as though they were a couple. Keith was not keen for that to change.

'I did what any sister needing an opportunity to catch up on payback with her larrikin brother would do – I got out my camera! Dad, even you will appreciate they are the best pics ever. Keith was scowling, shaking his right fist silently, unable to make a move or swear. Chloe was in a deep sleep, drooling on his chest.' Keith looks relieved when Chloe does not get upset. Hearing this news again and this time from Sheila has Chloe looking puzzled and intrigued.

Keith cannot keep from smiling at his sister recalling her antics, shaking his head at Sheila's face lit up with pure animation.

'I did mop up Chloe's saliva before I abandoned him,' Sheila charitably conceded, as though she should win Brownie points.

'Tell them the rest, sis. Don't bail out now that you have incriminated yourself,' smirked Keith.

'Well, I might have sent him a picture to taunt him every hour … and I might have told him I had sent them to Mum and Dad,' Sheila confessed, eyeing Chloe.

'But I don't own any white satin nighties,' frowns Chloe, uncertainly shooting Keith a sideways look.

Sheila reached into her back pocket to fetch her phone.

'Well, whose was this, then?' Sheila asked, showing Chloe her phone gallery pictures.

'Oh, oh … now I remember! Jill was doing her photography

assignment on nocturnal shots and avoiding red eye reflections. I had been posing for her, wearing one of Gabby's nighties and hugging this big teddy bear Jill had brought as a prop. After that grass skirt drama, I was definitely not going outside again,' Chloe added, shaking her head and biting her lower lip.

'Yes, that was bloody hilarious. Mum, can you imagine my smitten brother opening the door to discover Chloe in a grass bra, grass skirt and grass slippers? She had her bikini on underneath, and was still holding the champagne glass that Jill had her sipping from. Jill was doing her photography assignment when the wind blew the door shut. They were both in a frenzy to get the keys for their unit again before their dinner burnt on the stove.'

'I wish I could have seen that printed pic,' Keith said in a deep sexy timbre. 'Where is that pic, Miss Chloe?' Keith began tickling her. 'Did you get a copy of that pic, sis?'

'Now we will have no more tales of Chloe's misadventures, you pair. I'm outnumbered here', she said, shyly moving to hold Keith's hand.

'Well, now, are you going to date my brother?' persisted Sheila.

Chloe and Keith both smiled facing each other, prolonging their eye contact. Keith moved closer, giving Chloe a warm bony hug.

'It would be an exclusive deal, just you and the white satin lady,' he joked.

Chloe hugged Keith shyly, ducking her head, sensing all

eyes upon them.

'She nearly killed me my first surgery night, Dad,' Keith announced, nudging Chloe with his elbow.

'How so?'

'She was checking out my package all night!'

Smiling, shaking her head and blushing with her hand over her face, Chloe defended herself, holding his gaze. 'I was looking for signs of haemorrhage on his dressing. You had a pillowcase over your groin.'

'Well, I didn't know that. I just kept waking up, holding your arm.'

'Yes, every time I lifted the blankets, you grabbed me. You were off your face with fentanyl. You kept reporting pain and rabbiting on about the lady in the white satin.'

'Yes, exactly! Dad, you can imagine, every time my body responded, there was a tube in my old fella. I tell you, Chloe nearly killed me.'

Now, Lizzy, Lionel and Sheila were laughing so hard they were mopping their eyes and gasping for breath. Chloe ineffectively tried to hide her reddened face with the hand Keith was not holding.

'I was trying to keep his other hand still, to get a good trace on the arterial line in his left wrist that was recording his blood pressure on the monitor with every pulse. I was weaning him off the noradrenaline drug as his blood pressure improved,' Chloe clarified.

'She was helping my blood pressure all right.' Keith winked at his dad.

Still mortified and hiding behind her hand, Chloe opened her mouth again to shyly defend herself.

'Keith kept holding my hand, moaning about his white satin lady and reporting pain. So, I held his hand to try to comfort him, but he got agitated with more mumbling and groaning. I didn't know that she was me——'

Sheila interrupted. 'Then Chloe wanted me to ring the white satin lady for you, as soon as she got home the next morning. What was I to say?'

'What did you say?' they echoed.

'Well ... I was put on the spot a bit, that hour of the morning. I had to stick with the vague truth. So, I told Chloe the white satin lady had accidentally climbed into his bed at a party, unaware the bed was occupied; that Keith had been a complete gentleman, keeping his hands to himself and that she did not know Keith existed, because he made his escape as soon as she rolled over again.'

'Well, that definitely was the truth,' Keith nodded ardently. 'But since then, the problem is that Chloe has been reserving me for this other woman.'

'Oh, you lot are a circus!' Lizzy laughed.

'So, he's in with a chance, yeah?' queried Lionel.

'Definitely! Even though he was the most exhausting patient. He wore me out that night, let me tell you!' Chloe nudged Keith. 'I could not leave him alone for two minutes. I changed tactics, trying to get what I thought was his partner's information out of him to ring her.'

'What did he say?' Sheila leant forward with interest.

'Just vague stuff that was no help at all ...'

'Like what?'

Chloe's eyes looked upward, remembering. '"She's lovely" ... "she's beautiful" ... I really like her" ... Now that I think about it, he was gazing intently at me at the time. I was trying to get her phone number, thinking he should know his partner's number from memory because Sheila had taken his phone home to charge it for him. I thought the fentanyl and anaesthetic had made him too vague. Then he would get another urethral spasm from the tube.'

'God, imagine if I hadn't taken your phone home, you could have dropped yourself right in it!'

'Then, when I mustered up the courage to ask Chloe to date me, I was in disbelief. Chloe reminded me that I'm smitten with someone else, because I'd been foggy headed,' Keith related. 'I was enthralled and falling deeper, while Chloe was holding back out of respect for my infatuation with the white satin lady, her competition.'

'He's got it bad, Lizzy,' Lionel noted.

'You can see why she enchants me,' Keith said, looking at his parents. 'I had a gallery full of pictures of this delightful girl giving me a cuddle ... that I'm attracted to ... that I cannot get out of my thoughts ... thanks to a sister who was no help at all!'

Keith leans across to kiss Chloe on her rosy full lips.

'Well, I knew how sick he's been, so I am trying to help him with his diet and fatten him up for his sweetheart ... trying to stop him getting too attached to me because he was so vulnerable.'

'Get a room, you two,' provoked Sheila.

'We *had* a room ... but it got a bit crowded!'

'Well, let me tell you I'm delighted,' Lionel said.

'From death row to the throws of romance, just like the Mills and Boons novels Nanna loves,' Lizzy mused, shaking her head.

'I'd have probably been the last to know, if it wasn't for Dad doing the five-metre dash up the stairs,' Sheila reckoned.

'Keith has been terribly sick, struggling to come to terms with being septic, anaemic, short of breath, in pain, sleepless, itchy and with his malabsorption symptoms. We just took one day at a time, really.'

'We didn't want Sheila or you both stressing about me after her ordeal, either. Sheila still needs time to heal, too. I wanted to tell you all, but I can't even say the name of this diagnosis. Are you going to come on Friday?'

'Yes, it will be good to find out more info.'

'I will wait outside this time, so we don't crowd the doctor. And you can all fill me in on his latest results,' Chloe offered. 'He's over the worst now, it seems, as he's not so breathless.' Looking at Sheila, Chloe elaborated, 'Regarding the inherited predisposition, you all need to know who has to have the antigliadin testing and gluten-free diet, whether it's siblings and grandchildren, whether all those who are thin, or have asthma and eczema need to be tested, or if any children need to get bloods done. You will find that Judy, the dietician, is brilliant helping with his gluten-free food substitutes. She even found Keith a brand of gluten-free licorice, which was a feat.'

'Thank you so much for helping our boy,' Lionel nodded approvingly.

'I did not remember much of that stuff that Chloe has told you. I just call it DH, because that is all I can remember. All I could show you is what I find when I search "gluten-free" and DH on the internet. But when I go to the chemist, "gluten-free" comes up on my file.'

'Oh, I see. You need gluten-free medications and mixtures too.'

'I'm too scared to touch anything with wheat. I seem to be so allergic that I ask for shampoos and everything to be gluten-free, milk drinks, the lot.'

'Yes, Keith's not absorbing calcium and iron, so he's been craving milk and meat a lot. We've been blending and juicing to increase his nutrient intake and adding gluten-free protein powder to his drinks, one of the products we got from the chemist.'

'These gluten-free Jaffas are amazing. Chloe even got me gluten-free Vegemite and no-wheat Weet-Bix.'

'Spoilt brat!' Sheila teased, ruffling her light brown brother's hair. 'I am glad Chloe could sort this out for you.'

'You could have just taken sick leave instead of resigning, though, and done your TAFE at night, couldn't you?'

'One of the problems that you have when you are sick and foggy headed is that when people confront you, you don't have the comprehension to defend yourself,' Chloe tentatively commented. 'There have been some misinformed workers having a go, bullying Keith. The dermatitis herpetiformis got its name because the blisters form in clusters like the Herpes virus, so some of the workers were convinced that because Keith's young, he has a sexually transmitted disease, while others saw the weight loss and thought AIDS. I know it's hideous. That was why Dr Strathdee made sure his employer got the correct information from him directly.'

'So that is what Barney must have been told. Don't worry, son, we have your back. We'll straighten Barney out and he can get the message out to the others.'

'I'm not bothered much, Dad. It was just another blow that landed well at the time, that's all. You know what it's like; it hurts more when it comes from people you think are your mates. All I did, Dad, was ask my supervisor if I could bring in a toaster. I prefer the gluten-free bread toasted. It's kind of a thicker bread, so it tastes a bit stale, like cardboard if I don't toast it. Next thing, Hugh lost it and said, "Fancy breads won't cure the clap" and he'd seen that rash in the war!'

'That's beyond the pale!' Lionel angrily insisted. 'Bloody judgmental idiots!'

'I just picked up my gear and left. They were all whispering about my dramatic weight loss. The smoko room went quiet when I entered too, like I was the subject of gossip.'

'Well, it needs to be stopped,' Sheila said determinedly. 'Pull them up this time and the next poor bugger might get some mercy.'

'I'm not working there anymore, so I couldn't care less,' Keith said, defeated.

'When people are sick, these large companies have

all these rehabilitation standards and protocols. It is the law. There is the Work Health and Safety Act and Fair Work Australia. Their rehabilitation officers are supposed to be giving assistance with paperwork to allow you to transition back to work, to give you time off to attend medical appointments – and a safe environment includes no bullying.'

'Yes, even at work parties, the Anti-Discrimination Act says they even have to provide gluten-free food and drinks that are specifically identified. Under the law, they kind of have to treat an allergy as a disability. In your case, with a severe allergy, it is a safety issue. And a bloody ten-dollar toaster is not a big budget item!'

'I know, but I can't go back there, Dad. I am not a coward; I'm just not up for maltreatment. If I find another job when I look more normal again, then people won't know. I've even lost all the hair on my arms and legs – look!' Keith said, displaying his bald limbs.

'People just don't like "different". Keith's wasted cachexic appearance took them out of their comfort zone.'

'I don't give a rat's crack what they like! They can bloody well treat my family with respect. Don't worry, my letter will be assertive. We will get all the family to sign a formal complaint. They can get their bloody Human Resource people off their arses to deal with this. It has to be stopped; otherwise, the next vulnerable victim will get the same ignorant nonsense. I am also concerned about your reputation, Keith. This kind of slander can do a lot of damage.'

'You'll just get their back up and they will label me a troublemaker.'

'I'll get a blood apology for you, that's what I'll get. You mark my bloody words!'

'Okay, then, Dad. I really wouldn't want anyone else to go through that. I just need to save my energy to heal rather than fighting ignorance.'

'We'll be united, diplomatic and assertive. Workplace bullying needs to stop.'

'You and I will sign it with our professional qualifications, Sheila. And get Dr Strathdee to sign it, too, with his medical stamp. Then the Human Resource people can email the complaint around to all the workers. That will raise their awareness, that when they have employees critically ill enough to be admitted to Intensive Care, they need to be provided with support during their recovery. Hopefully, the next "alien" that comes along will be treated with a bit more tolerance and mercy,' Chloe suggested. 'We will do it in a way that it will help and not harm. We don't have to mention specific individuals. We just need to address this unacceptable belittling behaviour and encourage this company to protect their unwell employees. You should not have to resign to get fair play, Keith. Sheila, we could write that, after Keith overcame serious challenges like a gangrenous appendix, anaemia, iron deficiency, breathlessness, malabsorption and his weight plummeting to 55 kg, he deserved empathy.'

'Respect is an expectation, not a privilege. I won't stand for my boy being victimised like that,' Lizzy reinforced.

'All right, just don't mention any of the worker's names. That's all I ask.'

'"Fancy breads won't cure the clap" isn't banter, Keith. It was demeaning. You don't deserve to be treated like that'.

'Derogatory!'

'Absurd!'

'Offensive! I probably would have wanted to snot someone, demeaning me like that. I guess we should be glad you walked away with grace.'

'You did right, son, removing yourself from the provocation. I'm so proud of you.'

'I know you must feel pretty low at the moment, but we are always proud of you.'

'Oh, Mummy,' Keith teased, moving in to hug her.

'Spoilt brat!' Sheila taunted, ruffling his brittle dry hair again.

Before settling back into his chair, Keith picked up lovely Chloe, hugging her confidently and sitting her in his lap as Lionel hooted in approval.

'See? Perfect day all round,' Keith exclaimed, looking down. 'Got my girl – and my white satin mistress – had my impish sister squirming and Mum and dad gate crashing my bedroom rescuing number one son off death row'.

Chloe silently moved in closer, strengthening her hug, as Keith bent to kiss the top of her head.

'What do your parents do, Chloe?' Lionel asked.

Sheila and Keith shook their heads vigorously, signalling not to go there.

But Chloe said, 'My dad worked in the railway. My parents have both died.'

'Oh, I am sorry to hear that,' Lionel sympathised.

'I have two brothers and a sister. My eldest brother, Jake, is an accountant. My sister, Vera, is a mother of seven and my little brother, Georgie, is in the RAAF,' continued Chloe, unaware of the eye language and grimaces warning Lionel and Lizzy to abort the topic.

'You shall have to come over one day and play with Julian, Keith's cute, little, white, long-haired Chihuahua puppy,' invited Lizzy. 'Keith nicknamed him the "Maggot" because he's white, wriggles and is attracted to meat.'

'Julian has these tiny milk teeth that are as sharp as needles,' recalled Sheila. 'And my pet Rosie is a cute little tan and white cavoodle. She's nicknamed "Buttons" because she has a fetish for buttons. While you're cuddling her, you will find she has literally chomped half the buttons off your shirt.' Looking for pictures in her phone gallery, Sheila said, 'They are both really cute. I took them for a walk along the beach when I was home last weekend. Julian chased the waves out and bounced back to shore when they returned as though they were chasing him. Rosie was flat out excavating holes the size of an egg cup.'

'I'd love to see them,' Chloe responded gleefully, gazing at Keith. 'I love animals, especially puppies. They are so playful and radiate unconditional love.'

'Good! Then, that is what we can do next weekend.'

Looking at his parents and sister, Keith perked up.

'Would you like to get some gluten-free pizzas or Chinese delivered?' he asked. 'My shout! We have been experimenting with different dishes and pizzas once a week. You will be surprised how little you really notice any difference in the taste of gluten-free foods.'

'You both know what we like. So, how about you all sort out the order and I'll pay?' offered Lizzy.

Chapter 20

Johnson family conference

'She didn't say yes,' Lionel commented, concerned about his son's happiness.

'What do you mean, Dad?'

'When we asked Chloe if she was dating Keith, she did not answer, and Keith seemed to be trying to take the pressure off her to answer.'

'It's all very new, Dad. Keith's still very sick, as you can see. Chloe said his comprehension is out of whack, so they won't make any rash decisions.'

'Chloe's actions seem to speak louder than her words,' Lizzy commented, watching them both. 'They make a really cute couple, don't they?'

Lizzy was watching Keith and Chloe after he wanted to lie down. They were both facing each other on the same beanbag in the lounge. Keith had been raking Chloe's silky, nut-brown hair with his hands, fanning it out on the beanbag. Totally relaxed, they had both fallen asleep.

'Mum, Chloe's lived with Gabby for over two years, and in the nurses' quarters before that. She's not had any boyfriends in either place. Brett used to finish work and Chloe walked him up the stairs through their flat, through her bedroom, to walk along the verandah. Brett used to say that only books occupied her bed. Sometimes Jill stayed over too, doing her photography assignments. They often watched BBC movies together. Brett offered to introduce her to some of his single friends, but she tactfully declined. Chloe didn't say she wouldn't date Keith. She suggested that he needs to get better first, to make sure that a relationship with her is what he wants. We both know that Keith has no doubt. Keith's been besotted since that morning he woke up with her asleep lying across him. Chloe does not realise that, so I suppose she is being cautious. It sounded like they have spent a lot of time together while she's been on holidays, didn't it?'

'Chloe seems very genuine, though,' observed Lizzy. 'I don't think she would be this close to Keith if she were not interested.'

'Chloe will be very protective of him. She stops a lot of witch-hunts that some of the senior Registered Nurses try to ignite at work. I have seen her in action.'

'Yeah, well that sounds ideal after what Keith's been through.'

'Chloe is surprisingly tough. When we all had an infection control training day together, one of the cranky seniors, Kelly, was carrying on, trying to rally support with the other team leaders in the ICU to get one of the novices victimised in a pack attack. Chloe kept suggesting sensitively the other nurses give the new student support to help get her on track. Kelly got pissed off by Chloe continually trying to shut her down. She got aggressive, angrily shouting and pointing at Chloe saying, "I have a right to criticise anyone I want!" Without raising her voice, Chloe made eye contact with Kelly and assertively said, "And I have a right not to listen to it". Chloe had stopped the bullying and silenced her immediately.'

'Why did they both keep Keith's illness such a secret?'

'It sounds like they had been initially waiting for his results. You know what Keith is like. He doesn't like change. He always takes a while to warm up to new ideas – that has never changed,' said Lionel.

'Chloe would never invade his privacy, either. She would not tell us if Keith was not ready. That's why she asked his permission, to build trust. Chloe is supporting his journey to recovery at a pace Keith can tolerate. Chloe has been hinting to us all night that Keith's condition is not just about a gluten-free diet. She was subliminally advising us to go to these appointments on Friday because there is more involved. Chloe was particularly emphasising that Keith's allergic condition is part of an autoimmune disorder.'

'God, I was in such turmoil I missed that part! After Barney's phone call ... I was waiting to hear why my boy was dying. Then, I was hanging out to learn why it takes two years to get over an appendectomy,' Lizzy remarked.

'Well, as a Surgical Registered Nurse who is used to Chloe's mannerisms, I was probably taking in her guarded body language more.'

'I just was left hanging ... wanting Chloe to agree she would date Keith once I found out he wasn't terminal,' laughed Lionel.

'Yes,' Sheila agreed. 'I'd like that too, more than anything. But Chloe was saying Keith's anaemic, he's had comprehension issues, he's short of breath, he's only just starting to put on weight, he's overwhelmed after the gangrenous appendix removal was complicated by septic shock. And with skin biopsies, a new diagnosis he can't pronounce, new medications requiring weekly blood tests and a new lifestyle, Chloe's saying Keith is struggling with all that news. I get the impression that Chloe is calming the turbulence for Keith by not adding a new relationship. Chloe was very open about supporting Keith to learn, and about them taking everything a day at a time. Chloe was not answering because she was not putting demands on Keith or wanting any promises from him. And she truly thought there was someone else that Keith was attracted to. That would have kept Chloe hanging back, not wanting to commit or worrying about being hurt or rejected. Yeah, I can understand why Chloe did not think the white satin lady was her. When we often visited her unit, Chloe was always wearing shorts and tops as pyjamas.' Sheila's face lights up with a bright idea. 'I'm definitely getting her a white satin nightie for Christmas, though!'

'Oh, you two! You and Keith both can't help yourselves,

can you?' Lizzy chuckled.

'You've got to admit that's adorable,' Sheila smiles, looking over at the couple curled up together in the beanbag.

'Keith's clothes are just hanging off him, aren't they? His trousers are all folded in on themselves at the belt. I was surprised to see all that pigmented scarring on his knees and elbows.'

Sheila commented, 'Chloe seems to be implying that Keith is highly reactive and vulnerable now, and that he resigned from his job because, physically and emotionally, he cannot take anymore turmoil. Chloe suggested that Keith has no energy for socialising with either family or work colleagues at the moment. He was justifying not telling anyone what was happening because he feels that all this is too much for him to absorb. Keith is saying it is vital for him to just focus on his physical health to be able to cope with all these seemingly uncontrollable, new changes. When Keith's anaemia and breathlessness go, he should manage better. Yes, he is a bit battle fatigued. From his perspective this simple operation has magnified into a two-year nightmare of changes, which at the moment, he can't even grasp. Keith has been sleeping a lot with his bedroom door shut. I was coming and going with my shifts, just assuming he was still getting over his surgery. If he does go home this weekend, be prepared that Keith might just want to sleep.'

'I'll make his bed up and they can both lie down together. You said Chloe's still on holidays, so we could invite them both to stay overnight.'

'It was so hilarious, seeing you both impulsively bolting up there and bursting in on them.'

'It's been a lot to take in, hasn't it? I can see what Keith means. I'm not sure that I really processed much of it, either.'

'Just play everything by ear. If we put no demands on them and appear relaxed, Keith might feel less edgy too.'

'If they decide to stay overnight, don't be offended if Chloe and Keith bring over their own food. Chloe will be in nurse mode. While Keith is this fragile, I should warn you that Chloe will be less focused on socialising and hypervigilant to keep him safe, wheat free, pain free and not itching. The takeaway food tonight was Keith's way of socialising with less effort. Maybe, let them both decide for the next few months if Keith visits you both briefly, or if they want you to come here. Did you notice that Chloe is only allowing Keith two options for takeaway food at the moment? Chloe's restricting him to order either his favourite Chinese or pizzas from trusted sources to reduce the risk of errors while he's recovering.'

'She's a keeper. Chloe's pretty clever to be helping Keith sort all this. We will eventually need to learn all this stuff ourselves.'

'Yes, she is. Expect that Chloe will be very protective until Keith gets his independence and confidence back,' Sheila warned. 'I am going to have to research this DH more. (I can't bloody say it, either!) Chloe's guarding behaviours are alerting me. I am getting a very distinct impression that the threat to Keith is still present.'

'What do you mean?'

'Chloe is controlling Keith's risks. He gets only two menu choices, which suggests he cannot afford any mistakes. Keith' weight of just 55 kg indicates severe malabsorption for someone who is 185 cm tall. Chloe fleetingly brushed over Keith's symptoms, maintaining prolonged eye contact with me without alarming Keith.'

'So, you're saying we should be concerned for the next two years?'

'For at least two years. My senses are detecting an ICU Registered Nurse on alert. I will definitely talk to Chloe more later on, so that I won't stress out Keith.'

'What we heard was overwhelming enough. Now we have to worry about other family members at risk.'

'Chloe told us all casually, while distinctly locking her gaze on me to highlight, that the very busy surgeon, Dr Strathdee, is monitoring Keith weekly. Not only was Chloe encouraging us all to be taking this seriously, but she was motivating us to visit the doctor and the dietician. I'll have to look up that dapsone treatment too; that's not a drug I am familiar with. The third time Chloe held her gaze on me was during her conversation with us when she was accentuating "autoimmune disease". Chloe was drawing my attention to the fact that Keith has a lower immune system, and with autoimmune diseases comes a risk of other related problems. Chloe was pretending to scratch her thyroid gland, like she was pointing to a potential risk of thyroid issues.'

'So, these autoimmune diseases can be serious and not a quick fix, you're saying?'

'That's right. Chloe's usually always disciplined with her savings. Yet, she was not even concerned about Keith resigning. Chloe's lack of response to Keith's unemployment indicated to me that it was the least of his issues. Keith didn't care, and so she didn't either. Chloe's maximum effort was exerted on giving us tips on Keith's diet. She was showing us pamphlets, brochures and his gluten-free foods. Even the eggs that Chloe showed us were from chickens fed only corn, not barley or wheat grains. Chloe was specifically directing us to support Keith by learning this diet.'

'Well, we can copy those brochures and read them ready for Friday. We should write down any questions we need to ask the doctor. We might need to take notes on Friday, too.'

'Yes, I will write down everything Dr Strathdee says on Friday to make sure we keep Chloe updated on everything. Like Keith, we are all relying on Chloe at the moment. We have to keep her informed of the test results, like his haemoglobin level. Chloe will also want to know, for his malabsorption issues, Keith's iron count and calcium levels.'

Chapter 21

The letter

A signed letter of support for Keith was written to his employer, Thompson's Graders for Hire, addressed to the Chief Executive Officer.

Dear Mr Martin,

We would like to officially notify you that, on 7 April 1990, employees of your company made slanderous allegations publicly about our family member. Legally, slander refers to the verbal utterance of false and defamatory statements that damage and harm another's reputation in a libellous manner. Under the Fair Work Act, bullying happens at work when a person or group of people repeatedly behave unreasonably towards another worker, demonstrating behaviours that create a risk to their health and safety.

On 16 April 1990, your Workplace Rehabilitation Officer received copies of the correspondence provided by Dr Timothy Strathdee (surgeon) notifying them that Keith Johnson had been operated on, for the removal of a gangrenous appendix. When Keith's recovery was complicated by malabsorption symptoms and an autoimmune disease called dermatitis herpetiformis, further sick certificates were forwarded fortnightly, on 7 May, 21 May, 4 June and 18 June until his return to work on 2 July 1990. Further correspondence validating Keith's dietary restrictions of a gluten-free diet was also provided on 18 May from the dietician, Judith Plathe.

When Keith returned to work on 2 July 1990, it was within his human right and the anti-discrimination legislation for him to request his employer to provide a toaster in the lunch room, since gluten-free corn bread is more palatable when toasted. Instead, Keith asked for permission to purchase this item himself.

Consequently, having provided this medical evidence, as Keith's family, we are therefore livid that he was subjected to public humiliation and unsubstantiated accusations of having a sexually transmitted disease and AIDS.

Please take remedial action to ensure that this workplace bullying, slander and intimidation never occurs again.

Yours sincerely

Lionel Johnson (father)

Elizabeth Johnson (mother)

Gordon Johnson (brother)

Josephine Johnson (sister)

Debbie Johnson (sister)

Kevin Johnson (brother)

Sheila Johnson
(RN, BAHS (N)

Timothy Strathdee
MD RACS

Chloe Barnett |
(RN, Masters Clinical
Nursing)

Chapter 22

Slow progress

One week after the letter was sent, Keith returned from shopping with his mother and sister to discover Chloe having heated discussions with a middle-aged male wearing an expensive suit. The Gympie branch of Thompson's Graders for Hire had sent their CEO, Justin Hills, to pacify and resolve the upset with Keith's family.

'Hi, Chloe,' Keith said, greeting her with a soft kiss.

'Hi, honey,' Chloe responded in an unimpressed tone. 'You have a visitor. This is Mr Hills from Thompson's Grader's for Hire. This is Keith, his mother, Lizzy, and sister, Sheila.'

'Shall we go inside?'

With a plastic smile that did not reach his eyes, Justin Hill addressed his apology to Keith.

'I am very sorry that you have had this negative experience

with our company after your twelve years of exemplary service, Keith. We were shocked, not just because this event occurred but that you felt the need to resign.'

'As you can see from Keith's weight loss and gaunt appearance, he has been very ill for several months,' Lizzy declared.

'That would have been traumatic enough without the insults that arose. I have come here, with an apology, to offer Keith his position back in the company,' offered Justin. 'How would you feel about that?'

Keith dropped his head, wiping a hand over his face as if he was rendered speechless.

'And I have suggested that any offer of employment would need to be in Gympie, not with the Kilkivan branch,' Chloe asserted, 'as Keith needs to be living closer to the hospital. I also stated that given the circumstances of his resignation, Keith should have all his original accrued sick leave reinstated as well, for the offer to be considered genuine. Also, before Keith even considers the offer, he would need a month of sick leave off, effective immediately.'

'Another month off?' questioned Lizzy.

'God! I forgot to tell them again, Chloe. I'm sorry, Mum.'

'Yesterday, we had another hiccup, Lizzy. We were going to talk to you about it at lunch today. When Keith brought the groceries in on Monday, he had an uncomfortable ache and thought he had pulled a muscle in his chest. Then, yesterday in the same area, the pain was more severe. When I looked, he had got shingles, following the nerve from his spine around his chest to below his right nipple. It is just one of those viruses that attack people with autoimmune disorders when their immune systems are weak. Keith cannot drive at the moment because the doctor has prescribed Pregabalin for the nerve pain. Then later on, he will need to have a vaccination to prevent further attacks of shingles.'

'Is that why you looked upset about Mr Hill's job offer?' queried Keith.

'I wasn't cranky, Keith. I told Mr Hills the truth. What Mr Hills is suggesting is not possible,' alleged Chloe. 'Most people with autoimmune disorders cannot do shiftwork safely. Mr Hills said that he can only offer you evening shifts from 4 pm to midnight if you wanted to work in Gympie'.

'Can't I?' Keith replied, looking surprised.

'No, you already have low iron and calcium from malabsorption. However, shiftwork causes various hormonal disruptions that can cause a different problem, like iron transport issues. Essentially, when someone is as ill as you have been, your body can do odd things. As a protective reflex, the stress of shiftwork could cause your body to act like it is being invaded and dump iron to protect itself. You need a normal sleep pattern from 8 pm to 6 am, and it needs to be maintained. With a vulnerable immune system, you cannot do shiftwork ever.'

'And I was saying that surely those decisions should be up to his doctor,' Mr Hill insisted.

Lizzy piped up. 'Sheila and Chloe are both Registered Nurses,' and as Sheila nodded in affirmation, 'I can tell that

Sheila agrees with Chloe.'

'Yes, if you are offering my brother a job, before Keith will even consider it, it must be daytime and with no more than eight hours of work.'

'It has taken Keith months to get his weight from 55 kg to 63 kg, whereas for his height, his minimum weight should be 72 kg. His red cell count has climbed from 100g/L to 120g/L but it should be 140 –160g/L. His iron and calcium levels are still low, but no longer at critical values,' Chloe factually stated.

'Sorry,' Mr Hills evasively responded. 'My offer was meant kindly. However, I am recognising my ignorance is the problem here. I thought this was a dietary issue, but you are saying Keith has another disorder. Can you please tell me more about Keith's condition, so we can see if it is possible for us to accommodate his needs? I am not really familiar with a lot of medical terms, but I would like to help Keith stay employed with us if we can.'

Because the militant Chloe had defended and protected her brother admirably, Sheila recognised that the conversation had reached a turning point, but in the end, no decision was reached. Recognising that Keith did indeed have non-negotiable health requirements, Justin Hills left to investigate whether he had any flexibility in modifying his rosters. Before leaving, Sheila and Lizzy appreciated Justin's personal comments to Keith.

Acknowledging his 'reliability and unblemished record of service' with the company, Justin reassured Keith, 'I would like to make a position available for you in Gympie, if I can. Our company values your skills, knowledge and experience. If I can't, we will certainly provide you with a glowing reference,' he said, firmly shaking Keith's hand. 'I also hope your health improves, Keith. I am glad to see you are in such capable hands,' Justin stated, nodding to Lizzy, Sheila and Chloe.

After waving Justin goodbye, Chloe tenderly reassured Keith that his comprehension was not deteriorating again. Chloe explained to Lizzy that, this time, Keith's memory loss is a side effect of the Pregabalin he was taking for the neuropathic shingles pain.

'I worry whether all these dramas will ever end,' sighed Keith in frustration.

'Well, like Dr Strathdee said, the dermatitis herpetiformis and gluten-free diet is lifelong, but after you stabilise, everything will get much easier. You have been on a steep learning curve and getting lots of frustrating complications, but they will settle as you get stronger. You have had to learn all these dietary changes while still getting over the acute phase of your illness. The main new thing for now, with the shingles, will be to use new towels every time you have a shower.'

Chloe tenderly hugged Keith.

'You're slowly getting where you need to be and, given that you are only four months along in a two-year recovery, you are making excellent and steady progress. Your immune system will strengthen as the malabsorption improves. In the last few weeks, you have not been as breathless, and you are now down to half a dapsone a week. Eventually, you will not

153

need medications or such regular doctor's visits. You will find your life will get boring again, just how you like it! On the gluten-free diet, your energy levels will be better than before.' Relating it to the mechanical jargon Keith comprehended better, Chloe said, 'It will be like a motor running more efficiently because you are putting the right fuel in the tank.'

When Lizzy hugged him, Keith suddenly jumped from shock as she inadvertently bumped his shingled chest.

'Oh, I'm sorry, honey'.

'I'll have a lower hug, Mum, thanks. Then I'll need a nap if you don't mind. Those new pills make me a bit sleepy.'

Looking at Keith and Chloe hugging entwined on the beanbag, Sheila experienced a fleeting moment of envy and grief. Lizzy silently hugged Sheila who was still clearly adjusting to her own permanent loss.

As Sheila and Lizzy went upstairs, Sheila said, 'I hope this works out for Keith; I truly do. They both make such a lovely couple. My concern is that this still seems a bit like a nurse-patient relationship.'

'No, honey, they seem quite close. I'm sure there is an attachment. They just have to wait for Keith to recover'.

'Oh, I totally agree. I love Chloe, she's a great friend and I have no doubt that she loves Keith. But from what Gabby tells me, I am just not sure if she will bond with a partner easily. Chloe socially isolates herself intentionally as a defensive behaviour, a technique that helped her to survive a traumatic childhood. I think we all need to make sure that Chloe feels like one of the family. It is really crucial that she never feels rejected.'

'Oh, how terrible. Chloe's such a darling. She is also just what Keith needs. They have a lot in common; he is fairly quiet, too.'

'For this to work for them, I suspect that we might need to be as protective of Chloe as she is of Keith. Chloe defends others well, but, having been a victim of childhood abuse, she tends to be less effective at shielding herself.'

'Keith will protect her. He's like an addict – he cannot seem to spend enough time with her. He will protect his introverted Chloe. Keith said he is really keen for a permanent relationship with her.'

'Yes, but if Keith tries to advance their relationship too quickly, she might baulk or panic. Chloe seems frightened about intimacy. The vulnerability of being in a serious relationship may be daunting for her. Chloe finds many people to be unkind and cruel, and I suppose many are.'

'Well, if Keith's going to be recovering for two years, they will have plenty of time to bond at the slow gradual pace that Chloe needs. We know Keith is always caring and considerate. I am just hoping after that kind of an interval, they will have united.'

'They seem perfect for each other in many ways, don't they?'

'I hope so. I love them both. Whereas Keith is physically fragile, Chloe is socially delicate. I think they will compensate for each other's weaknesses admirably. Chloe tends to avoid people who have hurt her. She does not try to forgive or restore friendships. Chloe is more likely to abandon difficult relationships as too hard. I reckon at family gatherings, we should not make a fuss if they pair off and smooch in the corner together. It is more important that they become a couple, because interacting with others like our large family could be pretty challenging for Chloe.'

'It sounds like we will need to give Chloe the support that she is giving Keith. If Chloe needs help socialising to develop courage and confidence, then that is what we will do. She makes Keith very happy, and we want her to feel part of our family,' Lizzy asserted.

'Chloe will love our dogs, as she bonds with animals more than humans. Chloe believes that animals behave better than many people.'

'She's probably right about that!'

'I am not sure ... but it also seems their relationship is still platonic,' hinted Sheila.

'It's early days yet, and Keith has been sick for most of their time together.'

'I worry excessively that Keith's illness could be the only reason why they are still together.'

'I hope not. They both seem to care for each other. What do you mean?'

'I mean that while he's sick, Keith's no threat.'

'He's no threat when he's well, either!'

'Yes, we know that. But this relationship is a big deal for Chloe. She does not know Keith like we do. She has to perceive that,' suggested Sheila.

'We might need to encourage Chloe to integrate with our family over time. From what Gabby said, Chloe has not had many positive experiences in a family atmosphere.'

'The trick will be to get the balance right. We need to give Chloe just enough attention that she feels welcome but not enough to frighten her.'

'At Christmas, let them mingle in a place that is not the centre of attention, so that Chloe will be comfortable.'

'You'll remind me?'

'Yeah. We will plan a few things in advance. We need to make sure that everyone welcomes Chloe without asking too many personal or background questions. Under all her layers, I believe that Chloe has experienced much more grief than all of us combined.'

'Your plan sounds ideal. Kevin, Deb, Josie and Gordie will be naturally intrigued seeing Keith with someone. Like Chloe, Keith has not been in a rush to find the right partner. They have both waited and been selective.'

'Yes, that's true. We can encourage the family to offer food at Christmas but pre-warn them not to ask personal questions. It would be lovely to see Chloe relax in our calm family dynamics and friendly banter, without feeling overwhelmed.'

'Our large family needs to envelope them, without asking too many intrusive personal questions.'

'Oh, and we should update them on what Keith has been going through by just saying he's been pretty sick and still recovering. With this genetics news, they need to be aware about getting that anti-body test next time they get bloods done.'

'Have you mentioned any of this to Keith?'

'Not yet. I will when he's better, I guess. I feel I need to tell him not to make any big moves. We'll be pretty safe for a while, I expect. Keith doesn't like changes, anyway.'

Chapter 23

The weekend at the Johnsons

The weekend at Lizzy and Lionel's was a huge success. Chloe helped Lizzy with Keith's gluten-free meals, and whenever Keith felt fatigued, he and Chloe withdrew to his room.

The puppies were a huge hit. Chloe excitedly patted Julian and Rosie, who were madly wagging their tails, climbing over each other for attention and bringing over toys to play. Julian would open his mouth and yawn if his ball was stationary too long. Rosie bounded out of the main bedroom with a roll of Lizzy's yarn as if she had found a new treasure. After going into the kitchen to find a chicken treat to exchange for Lizzy's wool ball, Keith returned to find Chloe giggling. Julian was playing tug of war, with her hair tie firmly entrenched in his teeth, digging his front paws in for leverage and arching his head backwards, with the hair tie stretched against Chloe's fingers.

Julian showed no signs of wanting to relinquish his prize.

'I had my head down rubbing Rosie's belly, trying to get the wool out of her gob,' she laughed. 'Julian got up on his hind legs and slid that tie right off my ponytail, quick as anything.'

Each time Chloe let go of the hair tie, Julian retreated further, remaining just out of her reach.

'You're a waskily, wittle wodent,' Chloe taunted, stretching over without success. Distracted by Keith squeaking his furry pink bunny, Julian dropped the hair tie and dashed over to fill his mouth with the favourite toy. Lionel and Lizzy enjoyed watching the exuberant puppies nibbling Chloe's ears with their milk teeth as she squealed in delight. Rosie then climbed nimbly into Keith's lap. As he picked her up, she madly washed his dirty face and neck. Keith laughed when behind his ears got a thorough good licking, as though he had not bathed in a week.

'Well, you won't need a bath today now, son,' Lionel commented.

'Not for a month after all that attention,' Keith laughed.

As Rosie jumped up, using her two back legs to attempt a further face wash, 'Have you missed me, cheeky chops?' Keith queried.

Rosie, unable to stay still long enough for pats, pounced over towards Chloe.

'My turn, is it?' Chloe said, patting Rosie's tan and white coat. Rosie began rapidly circling, trying to catch her tail, tripping over Keith's feet in the process.

'They are gorgeous! You two are adorable,' Chloe said,

rescuing her soft fingers away from Julian's milk teeth.

'You have a lovely home and property here,' she commented, looking out at the distant blue mountains shadowed by low cumulus clouds.

Lionel said, sipping his coffee contentedly, 'Yes, we like it. The kids can get on bikes and go for long rides when they want. The horses and cows love grazing in the paddock, especially down near the waterhole.'

'Have you heard anymore from that Gympie manager?' Lizzy inquired.

'Yes, Mum. I have accepted some part-time work starting next Monday. Part-time was all he could offer at the moment, and I am more than happy to see how that goes. I will start working Monday, Wednesday and Friday at Amamoor next week. I can still do my Diesel Fitter Course at TAFE on Tuesdays and Thursdays, so it's great.'

'And Keith will be getting paid as full-time. Mr Hills said that Thompson Graders will be paying for him to attend the TAFE subjects under an apprenticeship scheme. He said it is more productive having staff with mechanical skills out in the field,' Chloe said.

'At least you don't have to travel far and can get home every night, son,' Lionel replied.

'I expect it might be challenging to work full days again. Mr Hills understands that these arrangements will be just as a trial at first, but now I am reducing that Pregabalin medication, I should cope,' Keith explained.

'Well, let me say, I'm pleased they finally got their act

together,' said Lizzy.

'They say the shortest journey is for both parties to meet halfway. Since I am improving this should be a win-win situation for both them and me.'

'It's not like you were ever any problem to the company before you got sick, Keith. This illness was nothing anyone could have predicted. We still don't even know who in the family carries those gluten-free genes, though Doctor Strathdee did look suspiciously at me ... I'm just grateful that the company is being fair,' Lionel commented.

'Did Chloe's attempt work to get your sick leave reinstated?'

'Yes. Unbelievably, they even paid me for the time off after I had resigned as sick leave, too. Mr Hills was very apologetic, emphasising that those destructive comments should never have happened. When he heard I was returning to work, Dr Strathdee rang Justin Hills to make sure I get breaks if I get fatigued. The surgeon explained that my iron levels are still in the low margins of the normal range. Basically, Mr Hills said that I can go home early if I need to.'

'Well, that was worth sorting then, wasn't it?' Lionel said.

'Yes. I will do my best to keep the road works going if I can. Even though road works are often pushed time-wise for completion, Dr Strathdee told Mr Hills I was not to do any overtime in this phase of my recovery. This weekend, I am just having Pregabalin at night, and only taking paracetamol during the day for the shingles if I need to. So far, the plan is going good.'

Chloe explained. 'Since Pregabalin causes drowsiness, we

need to make sure that Keith can operate machinery safely, as well as drive to and from the site. Neuropathic pain worsens at night, so, while Keith still has nerve pain from shingles, he takes Pregabalin at night. Dr Strathdee said Pregabalin will be mostly eliminated out of Keith's system by 6 am if he takes the evening dose at 6 pm.'

'I am glad you have had such an effective team backing you, son,' Lionel said. 'This has been a big year for you with all these changes, hasn't it?'

'It has felt like trying to run a marathon with no fuel in the tank. There just seemed to be one hurdle after another obstructing my progress, every time I thought I was achieving.'

'You are looking so much better. What weight are you up to now?'

'Sixty-nine kilos and holding, Dad. As long as I am not losing any weight, Dr Strathdee is happy. He told me I have to take at least five snacks to work with me every day, as well as the protein drinks.'

'Are you going to be grading or grazing?' Lizzy joked.

'Both, Mum,' laughed Keith. 'Eating and driving the grader will keep the day and my stomach full. Working Mondays, Wednesdays and Fridays also works because Dr Strathdee's clinic time got changed to Thursdays. He told the hospital he needed to change his clinic times, because he wanted tests done on Thursday to get the results on Friday. Having the clinics on Thursdays let him contact patients to plan treatments like iron infusions earlier, rather than having them deteriorate over weekends. So the hospital swapped his clinic with the orthopaedic clinic times, which apparently suited both teams. The dietician is also available for appointments then, so I am only losing two hours maximum of TAFE time, rather than work time. I would lose an extra hour travelling if I had to drive in from the worksites.'

'I'm glad. That sounds good, son.'

'We'd better get moving soon, I suppose. It will be a big day tomorrow. We might need an hour or two to sort all these meals out. We should start packing our gear in the car and leave here at 4 pm, I guess.'

'Thanks for inviting us for the weekend,' Chloe said, hugging Lizzy farewell.

She rewarded Julian and Rosie with final pats before leaving.

Chapter 24

Sheila and Keith

On the following Saturday, shopping together in the mall, Keith and Chloe strolled along hand in hand, smiling and casually checking out the health food shops and bargain racks.

'Would you let me buy you a friendship ring?' Keith asked, seeing the jewellery shop ahead of them. 'I have been thinking all week that is what I would like to do with my first pay cheque.'

'What? No!' Chloe cried out, startled.

'You have done so much for me,' Keith said calmly. 'I'd just like to find a pretty ring and buy it for you to show you how much I care.'

'No!' said Chloe, suddenly hyper-alert.

The casual, relaxed moment was spoilt. Sighing a deep breath and trying to remain composed, Keith squeezed her hand for gentle reassurance.

'Okay, but I am happy for you to think about it ... There is no rush. You are just so lovely and beautiful ... I really don't think I could have ever coped without you. You're truly amazing.'

Chloe abruptly rushed to the toilet where she texted Keith, *'You go home now with the groceries. I need some space.'*

'I could come back in an hour or wait for you if you want?' Keith texted back.

'No, I'm okay. I just need a walk.'

'Are you sure?'

'Yes, I'm fine. You go.'

Chloe did not contact Keith for the rest of the day.

He sat in Sheila's lounge, staring at the television while recalling the conversation. Analysing every word he had spoken, Keith could not identify any aspect of his offer that could have been misinterpreted or have caused offence. Keith began pacing restlessly. Unsure of what he had done wrong, Keith was worried he'd blown it with Chloe. He could not eat anything when Sheila arrived home from her day shift even though he had cooked her gluten-free spaghetti bolognaise, to keep his mind distracted from his turbulent emotions.

'Everything okay?' Sheila asked, checking in.

'I hope so,' Keith said sadly.

'Where's Chloe?'

'In Unit four, I suspect,' as he quietly walked upstairs to his room.

Sheila followed.

'Okay, bro, spill. What's happened?'

'Nothing that I know of,' Keith sadly replied.

'Have you and Chloe had a fight?'

'I don't think so. We rarely argue about anything. I'm not sure what happened … she said she needed space suddenly.'

'Chloe's not like us, Keith. She's had a horrendous childhood; she is very sensitive. What happened immediately before Chloe said she needed space?'

'I wanted to buy Chloe a lovely friendship ring. I wanted her to pick out something pretty that she would like from my first work payment. I kept thinking all week that was what I wanted to do, to let her know that I love her. I wanted Chloe to know that I appreciate everything she has done for me and how much I miss her when I am at work.'

'And,?'

'And she suddenly started looking around frantically like she wanted to escape. She looked up, saw the jewellery shop sign and suddenly dashed to the toilet. From there, she texted me and told me to take the groceries home, that she needed space.'

'And you did what she asked?'

'Yes, of course. Was that the right thing to do? I haven't heard from her since.'

'I know you love Chloe, Keith. It is written all over your face. To have a relationship with her, you are going to have to take everything extremely slowly. Sometimes, I think Chloe has a post-traumatic stress disorder from being raised by an abusive aunt. From what you are describing, it sounds like

Chloe asked for space to regulate her emotions. Chloe has not felt loved and valued growing up, like we did. Honestly, I don't think she has had a relationship with many friends or people since her parents died. I think it was mainly Gabby, Jill and me, and we are all girls.'

'Obviously.'

'I'm not sure how to put this,' Sheila hesitated, chewing her lower lip.

'What am I missing?'

'Well ...' Sheila hesitated, looking at her hands. 'I'm a bit concerned that Chloe has been with you mainly functioning in a nurse-patient mode.'

'What?' Keith said, his eyes widening in surprise. 'She's been cuddling and kissing me the whole time.'

'Oh, I totally agree that Chloe's attracted to you for sure. I have no doubts about that. Otherwise, you would never have got as close to her as you have. However, there has been a lot of the familiar nurse-patient relationship too, which is normal to her. I suspect Chloe might need more time to commit to a boyfriend-girlfriend relationship.'

'Chloe can take all the time she likes. I want her as my forever person. There is no rush or timeline.'

'Perhaps you need to tell her that as a reminder.'

'I wasn't trying to rush her, sis. I wanted to buy her a friendship ring to show Chloe that she's important to me.'

'I think maybe that because you're getting better, Chloe's still transitioning to the changing dynamics of your relationship. Feeling loved and appreciated may be a foreign concept to an abused child.'

Silence, then ...

'What are you saying? That I need to remain ... what? A patient?'

'No, I am saying don't make any big moves. Let Chloe take her time to adjust to you getting better and to the status changing gradually.'

'What should I do?'

'Don't change anything. Give Chloe the time to make the adjustment, to transition slowly from you being a dependent patient to a friend and then to a boyfriend. Very ... very ... slowly.'

'Oh, I thought this was going slow?' Keith scoffed. 'Slow was the only pace I was capable of.'

'The friendship ring idea was a great way of showing her that you care – Chloe will understand that – but she retreated. That means she wasn't ready to process it or integrate more just yet. Maybe she interpreted the ring as implying more obligations?'

'So, what should I do, now that I have stuffed up?'

'Just to give you some background and perspective, Chloe has lived in her unit for about two years. Gabby and Chloe always waved and said hello when we bumped into each other, when we parked or saw each other at work. Gabby would come over and invite us to parties, or out to dinner all the time, like she did with the nurses in the other units. Chloe only came over for the first time ever after Brett died to check in on me. Chloe started bringing over meals, stopping by for a chat, taking me to work because I was depressed, like a caring nurse. Then, as I got stronger, I saw her less because I needed her less. When we did interact, it was different. Chloe was now more a friend and equal, and then the friendship grew. Chloe trusts me now. I must admit I was worried about showing her those photos I took without her permission. That could have gone bad, but it didn't because Chloe had built up a trust with me and understood that I would never deliberately hurt her.'

'God! I was bloody worried. When I asked Chloe out on a date, she told me that I was confused, that I was in love with the white satin lady. When I tried to explain the photos were of her, she wanted to see them. As in she wanted to see them to help me to identify the other woman, to help me find her. I panicked, not knowing what the hell to do. I was totally foggy headed sitting there, desperately trying to think what to say and do.'

'Chloe would not have wanted to see you distraught.'

'So, retrospectively when you think about it, I suppose you could say that I have actually been committed to this relationship longer than she has?'

'Yes. Thank God you did not show her the photos when your friendship was new! Chloe might have been scared off.'

'I know. That's why I got you to explain. I didn't want Chloe to think we invaded her privacy. You did it in just the right way. You kept up our usual banter and had her smiling. Chloe also understood that we had not shown the pics to anyone else too, except for Mum and Dad that day in her presence.'

'I kept the attention on teasing you and off Chloe so that she did not withdraw. I tried to do it in a way that she stayed to protect you from your taunting sister.'

'Well, it worked! I was truly grateful – although that situation was of your making, you evil wench!' Keith smiled continuing their usual banter.

'Maybe let Chloe come back to you, in her own time. Don't ask for explanations when she returns. Just appreciate that she is back and her emotions were unravelling. Until we know differently, just mentally process this interval as Chloe taking the time she needs to recalibrate where she is in your relationship. Chloe would not be asking for space unless she needed it.'

'I'm already missing her,' Keith's eyes watered.

Sheila hugged him supportively.

'And I bet that Chloe feels the same. She could be feeling frightened about what demands would be put on her in a more intimate relationship. The way Chloe melts into you and maintains touch with your hands indicates she cares deeply for you. She has been enjoying your hugs, which is a very good sign. We don't really know why Chloe's feeling scared. Chloe might be worrying whether she can cope.'

Sheila paused before elaborating. 'Many orphans and child abuse victims don't bond with others in relationships because they do not want to feel rejected or hurt. You will need to allow her to change those defensive boundaries she has erected at her own pace. You've respected her request for space, so smile and wave if you bump into her, but back off wanting to change the nature of your relationship too quickly. If she comes home with us for Christmas, I imagine Chloe will be missing her parents and siblings. She could get overwhelmed by meeting more of us. Maybe, just stay an hour at Mum and Dad's, if that's all she wants. Or let her ring her family from your room. You could offer to visit with her family too, if she wants. Go Christmas shopping if she invites you... gently ... slowly ... briefly ... if she looks overwhelmed.'

'As long as Chloe is never afraid of me ...' Keith mused.

'Chloe is terrified of people. There have been cruel people in her early childhood when she was powerless. Adults abused their power to harm her when she was a defenceless child, from what Gabby said, and that is my understanding too. Then the vulnerable Chloe went from an abusive aunty to experiencing many toxic dominant females in nursing too.'

'It makes me angry that people get away with doing that to small children!'

'Yes, it's awful! Years of abuse would tend to make Chloe feel socially anxious and fearful. It has stopped Chloe from developing healthy social relationships. You will need to be patient and loving.' Sheila hugged her brother to console him. 'Personally, I don't think Chloe could have chosen a better partner.'

'I have seen Chloe defending others from those in authority against destructive judgmental behaviours. Chloe stops them and shuts them down abruptly – but that is protecting others. Chloe develops overwhelming anxiety and fear when she is under attack. I saw that happen at work when she was innocent of the accusations being made. Chloe gives the person making unfair comments a wide birth, like she cannot be bothered dealing with them. Sometimes abused victims can worry that provocateurs could ignite aggression, if they feel too threatened.'

'What happened at work?'

'When we were nursing students, we had an afternoon where there were heaps of unstable theatre cases coming back. Some were in pain, others were vomiting, relatives were approaching us wanting information. Chloe was six months ahead of me, so she had to do all the intravenous fluids and antibiotics. No one got any meal breaks and no one got off on time. We got back to the nurses' quarters an hour late, after four hours rushing about trying to get everyone washed, turned and comfortable. Then bloody Nancy Campbell, the senior nurse taking over from Chloe, moaned about the bandages that had not been washed and hung over the steriliser to dry. Nancy reported the untidy treatment room and pan room to Sister Wilson. Sister Wilson rang the nurses' quarters, angrily demanding that we all come back and clean up the ward. Nancy was just being a lazy cow. She tends to enjoy stirring up trouble. When you add up the meal breaks missed and the overtime the four of us had worked, that was about ten hours overtime that was unpaid. So, some of us nursing students united, complaining vehemently about the unreasonable treatment and excessive workloads.

'Chloe retreated to sort out the mess. She just put her head down and had most of the chores finished before our complaints were resolved. Chloe took the easy route of avoiding a conflict that would have increased her anxiety. The other three of us used our numbers and backed each other. We got an apology from Sister Wilson. When Chloe got thanked, she literally froze on the spot and appeared speechless. Chloe looked defensive, as though waiting for more insults to rain down. When Nancy Campbell tried to apologise, Chloe felt so ashamed about the complaint she had made, I saw that she did not believe the apology was genuine. Sadly, the apology may have just been a façade too.

'Nancy may have been trying to save face after her vindictive accusations were defended so adamantly by all of us. We had her outnumbered, especially when the day shift sister-in-charge supported our stance as well. Nancy tends to habitually "race with the rabbits and hunt with the hounds". I noticed that Chloe had minimal interaction with Nancy after that. Nancy was virtually wiped, devoid of attention. Chloe lacked the emotions the rest of us displayed. We felt angry, exploited and tired. Chloe looked emotionally numb. Chloe was not willing to divest energy into Nancy, who she believed was manufacturing undue attention at her expense.

'Chloe would smile and interact with Nancy minimally, not interested in either explaining her position or initiating any friendship. It was clear to me that Chloe was deliberately distancing herself protectively from Nancy's emotional outbursts. Chloe's coldness has warned Nancy that her hideous behaviours and games are not how she will accept being treated. When Nancy tries her habitual bullshit, Chloe shuts her down rapidly every single time. As a senior, Chloe uses her power to protect others. She will not tolerate Nancy's destructive behaviours nor allow the novices to be bullied. I get the impression that when Chloe sees someone deliberately harming others, she is not at all forgiving.'

'I notice sometimes that Chloe looks sad. I wondered if my wanting to buy her a friendship ring challenged her low self-esteem. This morning, Chloe had been so relaxed and her usual affectionate self. When her mood changed so ultra quickly, I was left stunned.'

'We learn in our training that child abuse makes the victims feel worthless and despondent. Apparently, exposure to years of maltreatment makes the victims internalise their aggressor's poor opinions of them. They can feel guilty and ashamed from being programmed from childhood into accepting accusations that everything that goes wrong is their fault. Social withdrawal, depression and avoidance of certain situations like conflicts are typical behaviours for children who have experienced profound abuse. They can also be afraid to love and worry excessively about abandonment issues.'

'Well, I love her. Chloe is so cuddly and affectionate I cannot get enough of her.'

'Yes, we all love her in our various ways, even Mum and Dad. However, Chloe may not be confident that those feelings will last. Chloe sometimes experiences melancholy and shows signs of emotional pain. She does not believe that people really love her and want to hug her. Even when Lilly and I announced our engagements together, the other girls hugged us automatically. Chloe held back like she was chronically programmed to expect rejection.'

'When I think about what happened today, Chloe could have been emotionally overwhelmed. I did not see her face. I hope she was not crying.'

'If Chloe cried after you showed her how much you value her that would be a good thing. Crying means she is actually processing emotions and feelings rather than stonewalling. Feeling worthy would be an alien sensation for her. Chloe works really hard, doing a lot of unpaid overtime. She patiently teaches the novices to methodically set up for procedures in ways they can remember, to develop their skills. However, she finds it extremely uncomfortable if they return the kindness she has displayed. If the students and new graduates show their appreciation by complimenting her or buying her gifts that acknowledge her effort, she feels awkward. From your relationship perspective, Chloe could be worrying that if she commits to a healthy relationship, she could be rejected or experience severe emotional pain, as happened to me when Brett died, I suppose.'

Chapter 25

Keith and Chloe

Keith went to bed at 9 pm. While lying on his side, thinking about the events of the day and Chloe's reactions, he heard her key in the balcony door of his bedroom. Keith shut his eyes and lay still. He felt the mattress dip as she slid into bed beside him. When Chloe spooned him from behind, Keith remained still, except for moving his arm onto the hand embracing him. Keith was feigning sleep to prevent any awkwardness between them. During the night, as he usually would on hearing Chloe breathing in the deep steady rhythm of a sound sleep, Keith rolled over and cuddled her. Keith was delighted to have his white satin lady back in his arms. He found her presence physically soothing.

'Good morning, gorgeous girl,' greeted Sheila, pouring Chloe an orange juice, as though nothing was amiss. 'How are you?'

'Yeah, good. Are you on evening shifts too?'

'Yes, one evening, then two nights.'

'Me too. Let's just take one car then, hey?'

'Sounds good.'

'You having a juice too, bro?'

'Mmm, yes, thanks, sis. Did I tell you that I finished my first module in my mechanics course at TAFE?'

'Well done! You must be pleased.'

'Yes! I'm going Tuesdays and Thursdays around medical appointments. I can do all the modules from 6 pm to10 pm too, if my job ends up full-time.'

'How many modules are there'?

'Twenty-four in total. If I end up only doing four-hour evenings, it will take me four years.'

'That's exciting. Do you get to practice on our cars?' taunted Sheila.

'Yes, we learn the mechanics of simple engines in the next module.'

'Well, we will have to spoil our free mechanic, won't we, Chloe?'

'Absolutely!'

'I'm a sucker for a cooked gluten-free meal,' Keith confessed, smiling. Chloe watched on, thinking how attractive she found his vitality now that Keith was getting better. His sexy deep voice seemed to caress her skin, just as much as his physical touch.

Keith and Chloe resumed their affectionate relationship with neither party mentioning the friendship ring incident.

Keith was just pleased to have Chloe back beside him again. Learning from his mistake, Keith was determined to proceed more cautiously. He did not want to take Chloe out of her comfort zone again.

On their next visit to the mall, Chloe tugged Keith's hand, dropped her head so her hair covered her face and led him abruptly into an intimate lingerie and apparel shop. Keith was surprised to discover she was not interested in making any purchases. Chloe was staring over a lingerie rack, looking through the window at a thin wiry male who had been walking towards them in the company of two small unkempt girls.

'Who's that?'

'That pathetic creature is William Chambers,' said Chloe through clenched teeth.

Staring intently at the man's appearance, Keith was convinced that this William Chambers was the same person who had previously harassed Chloe in the local grocery store and car park.

'You obviously didn't want to run into him,' remarked Keith.

'Not at all. I walked in here because that tosser is not worth losing my nursing registration over. Willie's an impulsive prick with a long history of being a troublemaker. He picks vulnerable targets. That gutless wonder tried to strangle, Vera, my sister from behind when she was leaving him and had her hands full carrying her toddler. Vera and her sons will ring Margie if they need to. My cousin, Margaret, is a Criminal

Investigation Branch detective. When Willie was caught stalking Vera and threatened Margie, she towered over him, warning him off. He said, "If I see you again, I'll fuckin' shoot you!" Margie, who gets threats almost daily in her CIB work, said, "Well, don't fuckin' miss, because I won't!" Margie has won Canadian pistol championships, so she knew how to intimidate him right back. Willie was left in no doubt that she meant it.'

'Are you frightened of him?'

'He threatened me, but no. If that tosser ever tries that again, it is Willie who needs to be wary of me! The police charged him when the ambitious little prick assaulted one of them. To stop his nonsense, the big, burly copper lifted Willie by the scruff of his shirt so he could only walk on the top of his toes. When Willie tried to punch the officer in the groin, the policeman lost his balance and let go of Willie. He went crashing into the police van, and it was Willie's own stupid fault. The best bit was when Willie's legal counsel tried to use his single parent status to get a lighter sentence. The police prosecutor's response was that any judge looking at Willie's history should consider that his children would benefit from a break from him. My sister, who was sitting there in the front row on the prosecutor's side with a black eye and split lip, laughed spontaneously. Seeing my sister grimace and grab her busted lip, the judge gave William six months in jail with a direction for him to attend mandatory domestic violence prevention counselling.'

'What did he say when he threatened you?'

'I was going through the checkout in Brown's corner grocery shop. Willie was coming into the store. When he saw me at the checkout, he came over, intentionally right in my face to say, "I know where you live!" I reported his threat to Margaret. I also asked the witnesses who saw the whole incident to provide a statement. Willie behaves like he just does not know how to stop his bad behaviours. Unfortunately, all the counselling he received didn't make an impact. Margaret will sort out little Willie and his big man syndrome if he tries anything. My older sister, Vera, is a little bit like Gabby: they're both lovely but tend to choose terrible partners. Vera picks aggressive men who often drink too much, like Willie. She's petite and short, so they assume Vera's an easy target.'

'Would he have attacked you?'

'No, he would follow me. Willie is a coward who prefers to corner defenceless women on their own, so he can overpower them. He has been pursuing my sister because he considers she is small-framed and no threat.'

'I'd like to meet your brothers and sister some day when they are in town.'

'I'd like that too. They will be in town on 26 November. All my family is going out to dinner to remember the anniversary of Dad's death together. You are invited, of course; it's in our diary.'

'Jake lives in town, though, right?'

'Yeah, they have just had a small baby who has severe reflux. Jake and Wanda are a bit sleep deprived at the moment, so not keen for visitors. Georgie, my little brother, has just been relocated to Williamstown with Brooke and their two children. They are still in chaos unpacking, so I haven't heard from anyone in a while.'

'Would you like to come over to Mum and Dad's for Christmas? They both said to invite you, but we don't have to stay long if you prefer a short visit. I did not know if you were working.'

'Sorry, I can't do Christmas Day. Mary, who does the ICU rosters, always battles to fill the day shifts for Christmas Day. The nurses who are parents will work the night shifts to get the penalty rates, but most want Christmas Day off. I always work a twelve-hour day shift on Christmas Day to let the staff with children, spend it with their young families A lot of single nurses tend to work on public holidays and school holiday to make life easier for the nurses juggling shiftwork, study and parental responsibilities. Otherwise, they have dramas getting babysitters. Doing shiftwork and study is hard enough without balancing family responsibilities like childcare. I'm off duty on Boxing Day, though, if you wanted to visit then for a while.'

'I've got your number, Chloe Barnett – you just wanna watch cricket with Lionel,' Keith smirks. 'I will have to remember to tell Mum and Dad that I will come by myself on Christmas Day, and you will come and say hello on Boxing Day.'

'Thanks.'

Chloe hugged Keith tightly. The gentle pressure she exerted, with her hands pressing firmly in the middle of his back, pulling him towards her, filled Keith with a desire for more. When they returned to her car, Chloe passionately kissed and caressed Keith, leaving him with a sensory overload. Keith felt a deep longing to reassure Chloe about how much she meant to him. Knowing he had to refrain from expressing his feelings so as not to frighten Chloe off, Keith ended their hug by planting a final soft kiss on her forehead.

Intuitively, Keith sensed more and more internal conflicts raging within Chloe but he was encouraged by Chloe's current need for increased physical contact. To Keith, it was as though her adult desires were battling intensely with her childhood experiences of fear and anxiety. In this war, love and trust had to win if they were to secure a happy future together. Like Keith adjusting to living permanently with his new lifestyle, Chloe seemed to be enjoying her new 'normal', of having him present a lot in her personal space.

Chapter 26

Keith and Chloe

'We need to get that television aerial connection,' Chloe reminded Keith before they headed for home.

Chloe experienced an unexpected pang of jealousy when they were greeted at the hardware store by an attractive female security officer, who was smiling widely at Keith.

'Welcome home, honey,' she greeted Keith. Keith laughed, putting his arm around Chloe to introduce them.

'Chloe, this is Ruby, Gordie's gal,' he said in a fake southern accent.

'Keith, maaate....' Ruby bantered.

'Ruby was the door security here when Dad, Gordie and I were doing renovations. We all came in so often for paints, brushes, rollers, drop sheets, you name it. Now Ruby swears that we cannot drive past the store.'

'Lionel, Gordie and Keith live here, Chloe! They nearly have their own dedicated car parks,' Ruby needled him before her expression changed to one of concern as she noticed his trousers puckered up with a belt. 'Gee, you look like you've been sick, Keith. Are you okay?'

'Yeah, I was a bit sick but I'm slowly improving. Still the better-looking son, though!'

Ruby's mouth folded in a smirk and her eyes brightened with his cheekiness.

'You'll have your hands full with this one, Chloe.'

'Chloe's magnetised by my undeniable charm and is oblivious to all my faults,' he goaded.

'Well, nice to meet you and, knowing Keith and Lionel, I'll see you again soon,' Ruby taunted. 'And Chloe, don't let Lionel tell you that the hardware store security officer frisked him for pilfered property, then stole his son.'

'Okay, I won't. Nice to meet you too, Ruby.' Chloe smiled and waved.

'She's lovely,' Chloe said. 'I thought that pretty chick was coming on to you.'

Keith raised his eyebrows and smiling optimistically, asked, 'Were you jealous, Chloe Barnett?'

'Absolutely!'

'I'm glad,' Keith said, brushing her lips with a soft kiss.

'It's nearly lunchtime. Do you feel like going out for lunch?'

'Why not? Sounds lovely.'

As they entered the club, Keith boasted, 'I'm up to 69 kg now, I'll have you know. Mum says if I'm not careful, I'll grow a bum.'

Chloe checked out Keith's rear view. 'Low risk, in my professional opinion,' Chloe teased.

Keith tickled Chloe under her arms in response.

'Fancy going for a swim later?'

'Mmm, maybe. I just feel like a lazy weekend. I did all the cleaning yesterday so we could spend more time together.'

'We could go and see Mum and Dad again tomorrow, so you can play with the Maggot and Buttons again. You'll have to wear a T-shirt, of course. Otherwise, if you pick up Rosie, she'll chew any buttons right off your shirt and make my heart leap out of my chest,' Keith flirted, dramatically thumping his chest.

'A T-shirt it is, then. We can't have your eyes abandoning their sockets, can we?' mocked Chloe playfully.

'Would you blame me?'

'Well, I've seen you butt naked, young man.'

'And you kept coming back every hour for more!'

'You had a pillowcase over your groin, and for all your bold talk, you were the one grabbing my hand every time I checked your wound, like I was going to take advantage.'

'Be still, my beating heart,' laughed Keith. 'That tube making my bladder gladder rendered me utterly submissive, let me tell you.' More seriously, he added, 'I could hardly take my eyes off you all night. I wanted to hold your hand all night. I didn't know that you were taking my blood pressure from that arterial line. I thought it was just there for you to collect those blood samples you were taking.'

'I had to take a lot of blood tests to wean your oxygen and monitor your electrolyte levels. Your hand was so warm and gentle that I could have held it all night, too. I might have held it more if it weren't for you mumbling about your white satin lady. I was disappointed when I thought you had a partner. I had hoped you might be single. I was looking at your previous admissions, trying to find her for you. Then like a fool, when I asked Sheila to contact her for you, she was very ... evasive.'

Keith laughed. 'What did she say?'

'Something about the white satin lady never knowing you existed.'

'Well, that was true.'

'Sheila was really sheepish too, now that I think about it,' Chloe recalled. 'I was saying that this white satin woman was important to you, trying to motivate Sheila to call her. I was saying that you were babbling about her all night, yet Sheila was not a bit concerned. In fact, she told me I was not to tell you that you had been talking in your sleep. Yes, Sheila was thoroughly entertained, I remember now. And she was dismissive. Sheila hinted that the white satin lady was not in the picture when I told Sheila that you were seriously besotted with her.'

'Not was, am still,' Keith said, maintaining Chloe's gaze.

Chloe swallowed. 'I do want to be with you, Keith. I just don't know if I can do it.'

'Do what? What are you worrying about?' Keith gently coaxed Chloe, holding both of her hands before bringing them to his lips for a kiss.

'Whether I can cope with a relationship. I don't want to be hurt. I might not be what you need.'

'You are the only girl I want, Chloe. You are all I need. You don't have to do anything you don't want to, go anywhere you don't want. I just love hanging out with you. We have all the time in the world to just be together. I have no expectations that you are not already fulfilling.'

Chloe stared at Keith, challenging him. 'We both know that's not true, Keith. You will expect more.'

Keith kept his tone soft. 'If you mean sex, Chloe, our relationship will progress at a pace you are comfortable with. You can tell me or show me what you want and when you want it. There is no rush. I am happy hanging out together, learning more about you every day.'

Keith's natural, charming smile and genuinely caring mannerisms made Chloe hunger for more intimacy. She felt the restlessness of wanting more intimacy but not more vulnerability. Chloe used to feel safe being alone; now she felt lonely without him. At times, when embracing and spooning, their intimate body contact left Chloe squirming.

Chloe confessed, 'That's why I was panicked about the friendship ring. I was worried you might demand more. I am attracted to you, I enjoy every moment we spend together, but I'm not sure if I can do a romantic or sexual relationship. After my parents died, I survived by learning never to depend on anyone ever again. I cannot have my heart broken. I don't want to feel that sad ever again. I don't know if I could emerge from that depth of sorrow again without being destroyed. I am not sure I can survive any more loss in my life.'

'I understand a little of what you mean, although it is not the same. I saw Sheila's pain, and even though she was so devastated, she is still glad that she had met and loved Brett. I won't ever intentionally break your heart. I am madly in love with you. I will never take from you or your body more than what you are willing to give, Chloe. I mean that sincerely. When we do make love, it will be because you want to share your body with me, and it will only happen because you are ready. This is not a one-sided relationship. I need and want you to be happy in every aspect of our lives. I have felt a strong chemical attraction to you the first day you were in my bed with your arms around me. I lay there, still, for a good hour before you rolled over, because I did not want you to feel unsafe or frightened. Quite frankly, even though we met that strange way, I wanted to be with you from that moment on.'

'I was totally exhausted coming off four-night shifts. You lose about three hours sleep each day, and the more sleep you lose, the more crap you feel. I usually catch up that sleep debt on my first night off. I would have gone to sleep earlier, but Jill wanted those photos for her assignment. Then I thought, rather than rewash the nightie after only wearing it for half an hour, I would wear it all night. I was really fatigued even before Gabby started partying. They were so noisy that I thought, *I'm going to take Sheila up on the offer of her room again, or I'll go insane.* You're right – I would have panicked waking up in bed with a stranger.'

'As soon as you rolled over, I crawled out of the bed so that you would not wake up. Please know that as my love and longing grow, I will never act on it without consent. It won't be easy with the way I feel about you growing, but I will walk away to cool down if I must. I would never hurt you intentionally.'

'I would have been worrying about what could have happened when I was asleep.'

'Only you dribbling,' Keith teased.

'It must have been addictive dribble to keep you coming back for more,' Chloe said. 'Actually, in your narcotic delirium, you mumbled something about really liking her, but needing consent, or something to that effect. You were staring so intensely at my face that I thought you were disorientated. I thought you were mistaking me for your partner.'

'I just want us both to enjoy where we are at right now, Chloe. There will be no pressure. I only asked about buying you a friendship ring, because I wanted to show you that I really am totally committed to you. Buying you a ring would be a way of expressing my affection. I also wanted to get you the ring as a symbol of appreciation for all that you have done for me. I could never have got better without your help. You even made learning all those foods seem like fun and an adventure, when I was panicked and struggling to get my head straight. I missed you the whole week I was away too, so to me the ring symbolised us belonging to each other.'

'Keith, I feel attracted to you too, but I don't know if I can do this. I want to be with you, but I am scared.'

'Scared? Of us being in a relationship?'

'Of losing someone else I love, of being unable to cope with the obligations of a relationship, of being able to make you happy. I am scared of life, Keith! It has been twelve years since my father died and I still miss him, every single day. Sometimes just getting through each day is a big challenge for me. I hurt. Relationships are painful.'

'What would an ideal relationship for you look like? Tell me what a happy future for you would be.'

'No pain, maybe mutual goals. I would like to live in a home with a puppy or two. I would like to feel safe, so security systems with cameras and alarms would be important. I'm sorry I cannot honestly say much about living with you, because I don't know if I will like sex or going further than hugs, kisses and holding hands.' Chloe's eyes watered. 'I know I sound pathetic. I am not sure about a relationship, Keith.' Chloe wiped the tears spilling over her eyelids. 'I worry that I will disappoint you.'

'So, one day at a time it is, just like we have been doing. We know we have both enjoyed spending time together, getting to know each other. What we have been doing is making each other both happy. We don't have to please other people. We just need to make ourselves happy. We are not going to be slaves to other people's expectations. There is no reason to change what is already working for us, Chloe. You can let me know as your needs change. There does not need to be any pressure for a more intimate relationship. I promise you that I love you just the way you are. However, we need to be clear about one important thing – I am not interested in a fling. I want to share my life with you, to wake up every day beside you. I want to grow old with you.'

'You know historians say that the Australian pioneers cleverly picked the emu and kangaroo for our coat of arms because they were the two animals that don't walk backwards. I try to use that philosophy when we spend time together. I want to be with you, planning our future, not reliving my past. I like your idea of replacing my bad experiences with loving ones. I worry that I may be too broken. Whether I like it or not, those horrific experiences had an impact. However, during our nursing training, the psychologists told us that during tragedies, the victims heal better if they can find "the gifts that traumatic experiences presented and accept the lessons". They actually used child abuse as an example of how it can protect those children as adults by teaching the victims not to trust people. The psychologists said during their debriefings after terrible events, the victims of childhood abuse and domestic violence often adapt by developing resilience to survive. I do intend to create new beautiful experiences with you, but sometimes, I get in low moods where I worry that permanent damage was done to my spirit during the nine years of daily violence. All I can promise you right now is that I am willing to try my best. I want to make this relationship work. I would like us both to stay as happy as we are now.'

'I'm glad, because that is what I want, too. Every day I wake up with you, I feel so happy. I went from this emotional rollercoaster of wondering how severe my next belly ache was going to be, worrying how I was going to cope with that incessant, itchy, burning skin irritating me awake all night, to losing so much weight and thinking that I was going to die because every time I ate, I was in pain. When I was sitting in the car that afternoon after the skin biopsy, I was in the lowest mood I have ever experienced in my entire life. You appeared like a beautiful angel. You helped me when you didn't need to; you have given me hope one day at a time.'

'You were a pretty easy fix once the diagnosis was made.'

'Yes, but you are kind. You are compassionate and you are very loving. You could have bolted and said this guy's going to give me a more difficult life, he'll be hard work, he makes even going grocery shopping a nightmare. Instead, you were resilient. You took me to your favourite treat shop and bought me a gelato. I will never forget that. You gave me so much hope when that first meal didn't hurt. I was enthralled when you shoved that big gluten-free Jaffa into my gob, converting this nightmare into a fun adventure. You showed me courage. You taught me where to find safe foods. We researched gluten-free custard together. You wanted to get soft proteins into me. You cooked me tasty gluten-free barramundi when I felt like I did not have even two brain cells communicating.'

'We embarked on this journey one day at a time, and I am not done with it. I just need to warn you that now as you seem to be getting more serious, I will try my best. I can only try to make you happy, but I feel broken. I'm not like other people. I like you but I can't make you promises. Right now, all I can honestly say is that I enjoy being with you. So far, we have created some beautiful memories in the last few months.'

Chloe smiled and hugged Keith.

'Initially, I helped you because I cared for you, because you were Sheila's brother, because you had been my critically ill patient and because I knew Sheila could not take any more. Then ...' Chloe blushed, 'I got to like holding your hand. I liked feeling you combing my hair with your fingers, stroking up and down my back, feeling your body melt into mine, your cuddles. I like them and I like you, but I don't know about the next part. I might not like going further. I might find that destination too personal. Also, there are now other people involved. Your family might not like me. They might want grandchildren.'

'Lizzy and Lionel will want us to do what makes us happy. If you want a puppy and no children, that is what we will do. This is our journey, and we both need to be happy'.

'What if ...?'

Chloe looked away, trying to hide her face. She raised her hand to hide the blush climbing up her neck.

'What if what?' whispered Keith softly, gazing attentively.

'What if I can't share my body with you? What if I don't like it? What if ...?'

'If?'

'I worked in the Emergency Department one night. I had to do a rape kit on a distressed young girl. She was crying hysterically, saying her body had been callously invaded and she felt dirty and degraded.'

'That wasn't making love, Chloe. That was a sex offender abusing his power and dominance to take what he wanted. That's not love, Chloe, the love of a woman inviting their male lover to share their body willingly and gently. It might cause pain the first time, but it is about the intimacy shared between two consenting people that love each other for pleasure.'

'I'm not ready. I worry that I may never be ready! I kinda know what you are saying is true about the rapist but the sheer terror on the victim's face burnt that image in my brain. It was like another form of abuse I had never thought about. I thought about her a lot afterwards, how absolutely violated and defeated she looked.'

'That would have been terrible for a young girl. It should not happen to any woman, ever. I understand that you are worried. That is perfectly fine. We cannot change our past, but we can sculpt a beautiful future together. All I can tell you honestly is that I love you deeply and want to share our life journey together. I want to make us both as happy as we can be. I love where we are at on our journey. Nothing has to change. When we are children, we are vulnerable, and people and events tend to rule us and confine our choices. As adults, we need to embrace our power to make mature decisions that take us to the happy destiny we want. As adults, we get to make the choices we can afford. We get to choose the direction of our lives. While we need to process our past experiences, they do not need to define our future. I believe that life is a journey of growth.'

Keith kissed her tenderly and intensely.

'I have been saving up frugally, because when I was seventeen years old, our family home became an estate, sold out from underneath us while we were still reeling from Dad's death. I need a place to call home, with no strangers coming and going. I had always imagined my home having two puppies that played together while I was at work. I wanted puppies that would love me unconditionally and that I insured and protected in return.'

'Two puppies and a home it will be then, when we can afford it. We will both save up, because sharing that dream with you will make me happy too. We will still go out for dinner once or twice a week, because we want to enjoy the life we have now while we are planning our future. We will save where we can.'

Keith looked at the calmness in Chloe's face.

'What are you thinking'?

'Can we go home now? I'm feeling a bit tired after that deep conversation and my last night shifts.'

'Me too. Let's have a nanna nap,' Keith said, smiling openly.

As they lay on the bed, Chloe came willingly into his arms as though their conversation and his reassurance had disarmed her. Chloe lay on top of him with her weight supported by her elbows. Her hair hung loosely tucked behind her ears as she looked at Keith's face before pashing him in earnest. Keith loved having her soft chest on his and her body pressed so close, that his responded. To take his thoughts elsewhere, Keith tried to think of his clothesline, but his thoughts wandered to a white satin nightie flapping in the breeze, which was no help at all. Keith ran his warm hands along Chloe's back, finding her muscles so relaxed. She began breathing heavily, soundly asleep, as drool dripped down, tickling his chest.

After their intense, open conversation, Keith was eager for Chloe to help him give the Maggot and Buttons a bath at the farm. Puppy therapy sounded just like what she needed. The pups had floaty toys he always put in the tub with them. They would need to take an extra set of clothes, because they bathed you as much as you bathed them. Both puppies bounced on their toys and pawed at them as the floating toys dipped and ebbed with the water movement. Indulging Chloe's love of animals gave Keith a strategy that he hoped would help buffer her on Boxing Day in a house full of strangers. While as a couple, they might be both fragile in their own way, together they were strong and resilient. Chloe needed to bond with his amazing family network, where over time she would find herself well supported and very loved.

Chapter 27

Chloe and Keith

For Keith's twenty-ninth birthday, Chloe made a bold move. Combating her fears and taking advantage of Gabby being on annual leave in Brisbane, Chloe filled the bath with warm water and bubbles. She then texted Keith to come over for prawn cocktails. With the downstairs lights left on, Chloe greeted Keith in her usual embrace before leading him up the stairs into the bathroom. She had left the lights off in the dimly lit room, with just a solitary, scented candle.

'I thought we could make your birthday unforgettable by being in our birthday suits for the first time,' Chloe timidly suggests.

Keith hesitates, unsure. Chloe was chewing her lip nervously, crushing his fingers and looking uneasy. Keith hugged her, unsure if she was really ready. The low visibility in the bathroom suggested otherwise.

'Are you sure?'

'Just a bath and cuddle,' Chloe huskily clarified, attempting to mask her inner dread.

'Honey, I know you are nervous. We can keep our smalls on if you want,' Keith kindly reassured her, maintaining eye contact. 'I love you. If you're not ready, we don't need to do this today.'

Determined, Chloe silently disengaged from his arms. She moved into the darker corner to disrobe before stepping into the bath. Blended with steam a pleasant floral aroma was soothing his nostrils, Keith sensed her fear. Nevertheless, he removed his long denim shorts, polo shirt and undies.

'Where would you like me to be?' he asked tentatively. Chloe tightened her facial muscles, looking behind her shyly. Keith stepped into the water as Chloe scooted forward, permitting his legs to straighten on each side.

Keith soaped up Chloe's naked back, massaging her smooth soft skin in a circular motion to release the armouring in her tense shoulders.

'You are so beautiful and brave, Chloe. Don't be afraid. You are in control here. Remember, there are no expectations.'

'Thank you ... I feel a longing for you in my chest when you are not here,' she admitted.

'I feel that too. But we don't have to rush intimacy until you are ready.'

'Just a naked bath and cuddle on the bed for today,' Chloe clarified before nervously dropping her head.

'Lean back against me and relax. Let me hug you from behind.'

Chloe leant back as Keith kissed the back of her silken, dark hair. He traced his hands gently down Chloe's arms to her hands, folded them over her chest with his on top in a warm hug.

'This feels very special, Chloe. I like it that you trust me enough to be this exposed with me.'

'It's just a tiny move forward. I want to create some pleasant memories with you. All my life, I have lived with fear and grief constricting my chest, feeling empty ... Now my chest has longing – for you. Instead of seeking to be alone, I now ache to be with you all the time.'

'I feel that, too. When we are apart, I can't wait to see you again. I truly love seeing more of you, Chloe, and this is a lovely surprise.'

As Keith kissed along the length of her slender shoulders and neck with his soft lips, she felt the slight scrape of his stubble.

'I am going to turn around now, so I can see your handsome face and give you ... give you a closer, front-on cuddle.'

Chloe sat astride Keith's lap. She began washing his chest with the washer before looking up for a kiss. Keith noticed that Chloe was nervously trying to keep busy. Keith rubbed his tongue along her lower lip as their kiss deepened. Keith felt his body responding, as Chloe's head rested gently on his shoulders with her arms locked around his neck.

'At least I haven't got the tube in my bladder this time that you are having this effect on me,' Keith smiled. He kissed Chloe's nose and migrated his lips down to her ears and neck. 'Are you enjoying this?'

'Yes. I feel closer to you now more than ever before,' Chloe whispered, releasing the breath that she had been holding.

'I'm truly glad. You deserve to be happy, Chloe. We are going to replace all that pain and grief with love and laughter. I want to show you that relationships are only difficult when you have pathologically destructive people like your aunty in your life, taking advantage of your powerlessness. Together, we will keep only therapeutic and loving people in our path, so that we can be very happy – together.'

Chloe felt the hideous contrast between her childhood of brutality and being wrapped in such kindness. She had felt, day by day, as if her need for isolation and safety was being replaced with seeking Keith's physical closeness. Instead of fearing this intimacy, she had begun feeling a drive to seek attachment.

'It's about creating new normal, isn't it?' Chloe said in a reverie.

'Yes, it's like living our lives as two parts of a whole. I feel incomplete without you. You occupy so many of my thoughts.'

'Before you held my hand and cuddled me, I didn't ever imagine myself being with a partner in a loving relationship. You seem to be dismantling each of my boundaries, Keith Johnson. Sometimes, I feel ambivalent and awkward being around you. I want to be with you, but I worry about the consequences of the next level of intimacy.'

Chloe closed her eyes and rested against him, acutely

aware of every tender movement and warm gesture. Chloe was astonished at the deep feelings generated within her. While she found the gentle touch of his warm hands along her back stimulating, her emotions were in turmoil. She felt conflicted – wanting more, but afraid of rejection.

'My need is to be with you. I won't deny that, someday, I want to be inside you, but it will be when you want me there,' Keith reassured, pivoting her chin upwards so Chloe held his gaze. 'I want the long-term deal,' he said, his intense gaze never leaving hers. 'You are welcome to touch and experiment, as long as you feel safe.'

As Keith ran his hands soothingly along her oval face, jawline and into her silky, loose hair, Chloe's mind flashed back, remembering how the cheeks he now caressed so tenderly had once been slapped raw by Irate Irene. Hope, grief and love battled inside her expressive, chocolate eyes. Chloe felt comfortable and contented, though entirely exposed.

After a little while, the water began getting cold. Goose flesh began to prickle Chloe's arms.

'Are you ready for a warm cuddle in bed now?' Chloe invited.

She stepped out the bath, exposing her slender female curves in silhouette. Each draped in a towel, they snuggled under the doona before removing their towels as they became warmer.

'I love feeling your naked body this close to mine,' Chloe commented.

She had never really felt pretty, until Chloe saw the

genuine admiration in Keith's eyes. He was delighted that Chloe was so relaxed. His cheeks practically ached from smiling and kissing her.

'You bewitch me, Chloe, mind, body and soul. Every day, my love for you blossoms to new unexpected heights. You are addictive. What made you decide to do this today? You looked very nervous.'

'I decided that healing from my childhood traumas required me to take back my power. Like you said, I was the one who needed to be determining my future. I don't want to be Irate Irene's victim anymore. You make me happy. I need to live, looking forward cheerfully rather than fearfully.'

'You are so brave and smart. Do you feel more relaxed now?'

'Yes, not so exposed hiding under covers.'

'Mmm, but you are still delightfully naked,' Keith taunted, rubbing splayed hands up and down her bare back.

'Are you hungry? I have some prawn cocktails made up in the fridge and a bacon, scallop and avocado pizza ready to pop in the oven.'

'Sounds delicious,' Keith said, nibbling her neck, giving Chloe goose bumps from this warm breath.

'The curtains are closed downstairs, so I can go down and get the cocktails and put the pizza in the oven with the towel wrapped around me.'

'I'll come too and bring up drinks.'

Keith leant over, giving Chloe another longing kiss.

Chapter 28

Irate Irene's reckoning

'I still can't shake this feeling that something extraordinary happened today to you,' I ask out of curiosity, wondering why Chloe was suddenly keen to progress our relationship.

'Yesterday … kind of.'

'What happened?'

'My Uncle Ross had a heart attack and was admitted to intensive care.'

'Oh, Chloe, I'm sorry to hear that. Is he okay?'

'Yeah, he has survived; he's fine. The real gift for me was, for the first time ever, seeing Irate Irene through adult eyes. I had not seen her for over fifteen years. Watching her manipulative antics, I could not help but realise what a dismal excuse for an adult she was. I know that sounds harsh, but it is true.'

'What did she say? What did she do?' I asked anxiously.

'The funny thing was that, in terms of the dynamics, her actions were nothing unusual for her. When Irate Irene got up on her religious zealot high horse, the adult in me witnessed what a brainless fool she is. After Dr Townsend spent about ten minutes describing to her my uncle's test results and the treatment he was receiving to manage his heart attack, her comment was "he's just constipated".'

'You're kidding?'

'No, I'm not, I'm serious. It was beyond bizarre her thinking someone would be admitted to an intensive care unit for constipation. Then, after she left the relatives' conference room, instead of walking around the nurses' station, she stormed straight towards me. Irene was yelling that I was worthless, in her usual "holier than thou", "shame and guilt" mantra.'

'Good God! What did you do?'

'Irate Irene looked angry from the news she had just received. Maybe her lack of control over the situation triggered her aggression too. She was advancing towards me with the intention of striking me. She wanted to rant and berate me with an audience watching, like she did when her congregation gave her unwarranted attention for her bad behaviour. What she got was security officers assisting her to leave the hospital premises. They informed her they would contact the police and charge her.'

'Good on you!'

'No, it wasn't my call. An intensive care unit is not the place for skirmishes. Irate Irene got the dressing-down she deserved. All her children except two have left town and have little to do with her. I gave her truth and honesty. I told Irate Irene she needed to mend her ways if she wanted a relationship with her children and grandchildren. Not one of them cares for her unconscionable behaviours.'

'Oh, how did she respond to that?'

'Initially, she kept coming towards me with the intention of slapping my face. She was totally unprepared when I stepped forward, invading her space, to keep her away from my patient.'

'Good for you! But you would have thought that her first response would have been to check on her husband.'

'Not Irate Irene! I'm sure the news about my uncle's heart attack would have made her feel as though she was losing control. The sight of me triggered her dominance behaviours and violent tendencies. The difference was that I am not a child anymore and did not recoil like one.'

'Well, I am proud of you!'

'I would not have hit her. I would have raised my arms to fend off her attack, like I have learned to react in my self-defence classes. I got the impression that it was the first time in her life that she had got a negative response to her pathological coping mechanisms. One of the male nurses, Steve, told her to treat the ICU staff with respect or she would not be permitted inside the unit again. Steve's tall, well above her eye level, and solid and strong. He was intentionally dominating her in both power and stature. He deliberately positioned himself between Irate Irene and me to protect me. When she could not get past him, she unleashed her verbal vitriol on him, shouting and displaying the behaviour of an alley cat. Rather than give her the attention she craved, he looked down at Irene, then told security to "get her out of here" with a tone of undisguised contempt. In a belittling tone, Steve informed her that it was an *adult* ICU and therefore we would not welcome anyone incapable of behaving like an adult. When Irate Irene, now in her seventies, went to burr up at him, two hands from security grabbed her arms. She found herself being forcibly escorted to the footpath. When she continued shouting that she intended to report security to the police, in her usual power games, she was informed that six witnesses were willing to submit statements about her disgraceful conduct. The security officers rang me to tell me that they had threatened Irene with charges of being a public nuisance and attempting to cause me grievous bodily harm. It was like her anticipated power base had flipped on its axis. Irate Irene was on my turf and her bad behaviour was stopped abruptly.'

'Well, that event sounds like it was very therapeutic for you. It seems like an encounter where Irate Irene and her aggression were not tolerated, was somewhat healing.'

'Strangely, I know it sounds odd, but it was a pivotal moment. I went from living in fear and dread, as I had been, to seeing her as a pathetic creature not in possession of any emotional intelligence. Perhaps it was being at work and in my uniform that permitted me to see Irate Irene through my professional eyes. I saw her as a criminal who operated from an emotional rather than a logical plane.'

'I'm glad that terrible incident was empowering for you,' I say, embracing Chloe in a hug.

'Yes, it was. I felt truly supported. When another two staff in the beds beside my ventilated patient came over, Irene was initially relishing an audience to denigrate me publicly. It was like a miracle when they jeered, contemptuously telling security to "get her out of here".'

'Disapproval and public condemnation were all the attention she deserved!'

'It was probably because I was at work that I noticed the contrast. I was using my energy constructively, while she was destructive. Irate Irene was the child having the tantrum, needing her absurd behaviours interrupted and learning that unacceptable behaviours have consequences'.

'Well, I am very proud of you. That would have been trying.'

'Well, this morning, I got a phone call from Steve. After yesterday, the ICU nurses were on guard. When Steve saw Irate Irene on the ICU door camera, he met her at the door, setting the boundaries. Steve told her that if she was coming inside, she would be permitted to only visit her husband. He insisted that she was required to go straight to her husband's bedside and behave. Trying to gain sympathy, Irate Irene demanded to see me. Steve said she was holding up butterscotch lollies, claiming to have brought them in for me! Irate Irene was excusing her conduct by claiming to have been overwrought yesterday. Recognising she was a manipulative cow, Steve told me that he told her through gritted teeth that no one was fooled. No staff member took the butterscotch lollies from her that she was offering, even after she attempted to gift them several times. Steve told Irene that her aggressive behaviour yesterday was documented by security and a copy was inserted into her husband's bedside chart. Steve informed her that if she ever came near me again, I would access that report to pursue legal action against her. Steve rang me to tell me how ridiculous Irene looked standing there, waving butterscotch lollies in front of the door camera. The lollies were Irene's pathetic attempt to reverse the power gradient by attempting to treat the staff as children.'

'Butterscotch lollies?'

'Yeah, she loves them. Irate Irene ate them in front of us children all the time. I am under no illusions. Irate Irene would never feel guilty; she is merely an unscrupulous sociopath wanting to visit her husband. When the ICU nurses united, ignoring her manipulating behaviours, Irene was left looking like the fool she is. She was given two choices: to behave or get private cover. With the threatening conduct they had seen her display, the hospital was within their rights to refuse to treat her if she got sick.'

'Good heavens! Well, I am glad you had today off, and not just because we are in our birthday suits. I am hoping your uncle is transferred out before your return to work.'

'Yeah, me too. It was a positive experience. I felt stronger afterwards. I doubt Irate Irene has ever done anything kind to anyone in her entire life. She was always slapping my face because I was the mirror image of my mother. I learned as an adult and health professional that you can only victimise someone if they are willing to play the victim's role. To me, the butterscotch lollies signalled defeat. They were a sign that the calculating Irene needed to employ more devious strategies. Even the ICU director yesterday came out of his office to condemn her behaviours as shocking. He told Irene her abuse would not be tolerated. When Irene told Dr Findlay she was entitled to "discipline her niece," he looked around and said condescendingly, "Madam, I am not seeing any child in here. It is you who are behaving appallingly." Dr Townsend, who Irene had thought would sympathise with her after he had been discussing my uncle's case, told her that criminal charges would be laid if any of his staff were assaulted. When Irate Irene persisted, Dr Townsend reiterated that the hospital had her name and details should any further incidents require charges to be laid by the police.'

'I'm glad. That would have been embarrassing.'

'Only for her, not for me. The ICU staff saw a mad cow rushing at me with intent to harm, and then irrationally attempting to justify her dominating behaviours. Yesterday, the security officers asked me, for their incident records, if Irene was demented. I told them assertively that this was not a new behaviour for her at all. I notified the security officer that Irate Irene had a long history of viciously beating up defenceless children, and that she vindicated her violence using religion. I used my power to make sure that her atrocious history was documented, because Irene could harm other nurses if she escalated with her foul temper.'

'Well, that encounter has boosted your confidence, Miss Barnett,' I said, grabbing her towel before dashing up the stairs first. Chloe chased after me but, despite her quick reflexes, the towel tucked around my waist remained just out of her reach. Crashing onto the bed and wrestling, Chloe ripped off my towel. We progressed rapidly from playing to intense desire.

'We haven't really discussed contraception yet, honey,' I said breaking our fun to talk. We were lying side by side with me lightly brushing my hands along Chloe's side. 'I know you're not ready yet, but I wondered if I should buy condoms just in case.'

'No need. Since we plan to be in an exclusive long-term relationship, I have started taking the pill.'

'Oh, I didn't know that.'

'I was kind of embarrassed to bring it up,' Chloe said, hiding her face over my shoulder as she moved closer.

'That's fine, honey. I just want to be responsible. I felt I should talk to you about what you prefer, in terms of choices, to prevent a pregnancy. You can always discuss anything with me. You don't need to feel embarrassed. Anything about our intimacy will be kept private, between ourselves.'

'I haven't ever been on the pill before. I started taking contraceptives when we began dating. I wasn't sure whether I would ever have the courage to be intimate with you. I just wanted to be protected from an unwanted pregnancy.'

'That's okay. I just wanted to be prepared for when you are ready. There is still no hurry.'

With her guard down, my gentle touch began making Chloe restless. Our intimacy continued progressing slowly until Chloe signalled that she was ready for our lovemaking to be complete.

To Chloe's relief, not only had she enjoyed my touch but our intimacy had bonded us on a deeper level. For the first time, Chloe experienced a deep romantic love. She told me that her body tingled with desire, and she craved more. Chloe finally understood why I had said I had wanted us to be together always. Chloe felt she was growing socially and emotionally in the comfort of our maturing relationship. When I had not thought it possible to love Chloe more, she showed so much trust and courage that I found my affection continued to grow.

Chapter 29

Christmas

I f left to her own devices, Chloe would never celebrate birthdays, Christmas, or any other occasions. Celebrations were never something she had relished since the death of her father. With Chloe only being three years old when her mother had died, she had few memories. Chloe could only recall her mother lying on a bed and her father lifting her and her siblings up one at a time to be cuddled. Christmas time was always going to be challenging for Chloe.

Chloe had always existed rather than lived. Before Keith, Chloe had considered life was a daily challenge to be endured until death inevitably released her from her agony. This year, as usual, Chloe had volunteered to work, as the Christmas Day roster was always a difficult roster to fill. However, Keith's parents had delayed their present opening for the adults until Boxing Day, hoping that Chloe would visit.

'Hello, Nanna,' greeted Keith, smiling and opening the door of their childhood home.

'How are you?' Nanna said, smiling and greeting Keith with a bony but warm hug while taking in his paler, thinner features.

Nanna, who was always mindful of falling, looked down at the floor to negotiate her feet around the mat. Pointing to a raw chicken neck that Buttons had abandoned on the floor, she laughed.

'I had a double take, then, Keith,' his delightfully wicked grandma said.

'Why, Nanna?' Keith innocently asked, following her pointed finger to the chicken neck.

'It looked like you had been dismembered,' Nanna chuckled.

'You haven't changed, Nanna,' Keith grinned in approval, embracing her in another welcoming hug. 'Come in and meet my Chloe.'

'Chloe, this is my wicked Nanna,' jested Keith. 'Keep an eye on her. She's full of mischief.'

'Pleased to meet you, Chloe,' Nanna said with a glint in her eye. She pulled Chloe into a warm embrace.

'This is Pop,' Keith said, launching in for a man hug from his grandfather.

Rather than being sedate and frail, Pop announced, 'Have you got the cricket on and the beers ready, son?'

'We've got a new flavour for you to try this year, Pop. It's gluten-free.'

'Pleased to meet you, Chloe. Do you watch cricket?' Pop

queried, hugging Chloe and beaming radiantly through creased eyes as his grandchildren began instantly crowding around to welcome him.

'Yep, I'm an Aussie supporter!'

They all settled into seats in the lounge with drinks as the pitch report before the game began. Keith and Chloe were sharing a beanbag over to the side.

'Now, Keith, you know I love my Mills and Boon––' began Nanna enthusiastically.

'––I'll make sure I get you some for your birthday,' interrupted Keith, knowing full well that Nanna wanted to know more about how he met Chloe.

Lizzy watched, entertained by the banter.

'Come on, Keith, spill the beans,' taunted Nanna. 'We can all see Chloe is a keeper and how close you both are.'

'I told you she's a mischief,' Keith said, winking at Chloe.

'And Nanna doesn't even know about the white satin lady,' Lizzy said, tormenting her mother.

'Any church bells in the future?' Nanna probed, looking towards Lizzy for hints.

'Oh, I'd never be married in a church,' commented Chloe in all seriousness.

'Why's that, love?' Chloe has Keith's attention at that remark as well.

'I'm a citadel girl, Nanna.'

'Are you of the Jewish religion?'

'That's a synagogue, Nanna. Chloe said "citadel",' Keith clarified.

'My dad liked the Salvation Army. They worship in a citadel rather than a church. He called the Salvation Army the "Christians with their sleeves rolled up". So, if I ever get married, it would be in a citadel, because the wedding costs would go to humanitarians helping others.'

'Oh, that's a lovely idea, dear,' Nanna said, nodding approvingly, intrigued and keen for more information.

There was silence and smiles all around. Everyone was making Nanna work harder to get her Mills and Boon fix.

'Come on, you lot! At my age, I can't be waiting forever to hear about the white satin lady. I mightn't live that long,' she joked, looking wide-eyed, trying for the sympathy vote.

'There was hot competition,' teased Keith, 'between Chloe and the white satin lady.'

'What?' asked Nanna, migrating forward to the edge of her seat, taking the bait.

Lizzy and Lionel giggled, entertained by Keith's teasing.

'Well, Nanna, it was a difficult predicament,' Keith began. 'They're both hot, but the white satin lady didn't know I existed, and I've developed such a fetish for white satin ...'

'Lordie!' exclaimed Nanna, looking from one to another, unsure what to say.

'Well, you're just lucky you have a lovely sister,' Sheila smirked, tossing Keith his Christmas present.

Lizzy and Lionel grinned as Keith unwrapped it – a beautiful shiny white satin nightie.

'Perfect!' said Keith, enthusiastically holding up the delicate lingerie, 'absolutely perfect!'

Sheila, Lizzy and Lionel giggled some more while Chloe blushed.

'Can I show Nanna?' asked Sheila, enthusiastically getting out her phone after permission was granted. Sheila chose the most discreet photo.

Nanna excitedly pushed her glasses up on her nose and leant forward as Sheila swiped through her phone gallery.

'There she is!'

'But that's Chloe, isn't it?' said Nanna, looking up at the original.

'Yes, Nanna. It was better than Mills and Boon. I gave Chloe the key to my unit spare bedroom for when she needed to escape her flat mate's partying. Then Keith came over for the weekend. He went to bed early and Chloe, coming through the balcony door from the other side, slid into bed. The room was so dark with my night duty curtains that neither knew the other was there. When Keith woke up, he wanted me to rescue him, but it was too good an opportunity. So being the loving sister I am, I got my camera and clicked away, with Keith clenching his fists at me in frustration. As soon as Chloe rolled over, Keith snuck out of bed and Chloe had no clue he'd even been there. It was hilarious. And it gets better, Nanna!'

'Oooh ... what happened?' the curious geriatric quizzed.

'The next time he saw Chloe, Keith was in Intensive Care following his appendix surgery. He was off his face on painkillers, rabbiting on about the white satin lady. Chloe, his ICU nurse, was trying to find the white satin lady for him, looking for next of kin details in his previous admissions. Chloe was trying to keep his hand still for the arterial line tracing that recorded his blood pressure measurement on the monitor, to wean his medication. Keith was grabbing her hand, off his face on narcotics. With Chloe looking after him all night, she had to give him loads of painkiller because the catheter in his bladder was killing him.'

'It was excruciating, Nanna! That catheter nearly killed me when I was looking at the white satin lady all night. And I woke up, thinking she was holding my hand.' Nanna chuckled. 'Then she was looking at my wound, she reckons, but the blanket lifting went on all night,' Keith said, winking at Chloe.

'You had a pillowcase over your groin,' Chloe insisted, poking him in the ribs, her face blushing. 'I was checking your wound.'

'Well, I can prove God is merciful, Nanna,' announced Keith. 'I must have dozed off when Chloe was washing off all that brown paint the surgeon put on my belly. It had all run down into my groin.'

Nanna's face was animated and Pop was no longer watching the cricket.

'Aw,' Nanna smirked while Pop chuckled. 'That *is* better than Mills and Boon. How romantic.'

'You lot are a riot,' Pop said, cheekily. Reaching over, holding the white satin nightie up in front of Nanna, he protested, 'And Sheila, that's discrimination! Where's mine?'

'You'd have a heart attack, you silly old bugger,' teased Nanna. 'Your ambitions might exceed your capabilities!'

'Next birthday,' said Sheila with a wink to Pop. Pop grinned in delight.

'Too much information!' Lizzy giggled.

Keith took his gift over to Nanna. 'Knowing you've got "green fingers", we got you an indoor mulberry plant, Nanna and Pop', he announced, carefully placing the cellophane wrapped gift down. Fascinated by the novelty gift, Nanna removed the cellophane, keen to remove one of the darker purple mulberries off the plant to taste it. She tugged and twisted, trying to pick several of the darker mulberries from the plant between her fingers and thumb, with no success. Expecting Pop to give her a hand, she found him in stitches, gasping for breath and muffling his laughter behind both hands, with Keith and Chloe busting their sides.

'You suckered me again, didn't you, Keith?' she chortled, suddenly realising it was a plastic decorative arrangement. 'Oh Chloe, girl, you're gonna have ya hands full with this one.'

With everyone still folding up at Keith's antics, Nanna recalled some of Keith's previous pranks.

'When he was a lad, I pulled the mop through the rollers of my bucket to ring out the water. The mop had about five strings hanging on it. He had put Lizzy's buggered mop in the bucket and hidden my mop behind a cupboard. I thought I had broken my mop when I pulled a stringless one out of the water.'

'You love me, Nanna.'

'I definitely do love my boy.' Nanna smiled as she continued dobbing on him. 'When he was a teenager doing welding at school, Keith practiced welding, with Pop teaching him, in the shed. Our neighbour, June, saw what they were doing and asked Keith if he could weld a bed frame for them that broke when they had visitors. June's brother-in-law, being an obese chap, had bent the bed legs because the frame, made only of inch-by-inch boxing, did not take his heavy weight. Keith did a brilliant job. But when he handed the frame back over the fence to June, Keith said to June accusingly, "Now you take it easy on Bill." I accidently spat out my teeth, June went beetroot-red and we all killed ourselves laughing. She still asks how the "cheeky bugger" is. Then last Christmas, he played a prank on Pop while they were watching the cricket. Keith was getting Pop non-alcoholic beers that were actually soft drinks. The bottles were practically identical; only the caps were a different colour. He drank two beers, before he twigged. That was why Pop was asking him if he had the beers ready today.'

'Sounds like I will have to watch him, Nanna.'

'So, what did Keith get you for Christmas, Chloe?' Nanna asks.

'A piece of paper and a picture,' replied Keith.

'He's winding me up, isn't he?' Nanna said, still intent on living vicariously through her grandchildren.

'Yes.' Chloe sat up, showing Nanna her phone gallery. He has put a deposit on some jewellery until I pick which one I prefer. 'Keith likes this set of a matching Ceylon sapphire ring and earrings and Sheila likes the pearl matching set.'

'Oh, they are both very beautiful, dear,' said Nanna. 'Will

it be an engagement ring or a friendship ring?' The room became silent as the individual chatter stopped, awaiting Chloe's reply.

'It's a beautiful ring for my lovely lady, for now. We will specify the rest later,' asserted Keith, not wanting Chloe to be put on the spot. 'There has been so much stress with surgery, the new diagnosis and then those painful shingles, Nanna. We are both happy for now, Nanna, just being together. We've decided to leave the labels that define our relationship up in the air for a little while. We have enough turmoil just learning my diet and getting my symptoms like the weight loss, anaemia and iron issues sorted. The malabsorption has caused me some problems with comprehension and concentration. I need to get off the dapsone medication too.'

'I understand,' sympathised Nanna. 'It is very sensible for you both to just take your time. It has all been a huge upheaval for you. You've had such a dramatic year, really. I remember when Lizzy and Lionel told me they had got the fright of their lives after receiving a phone call with someone telling them you were dying from a blood transfusion. They told me that when they rushed over to Sheila's, the first thing they saw was how much weight you had lost. Even when you clarified the correct diagnosis, they remained seriously concerned about you being so thin, anaemic and short of breath. We were all so worried about you having such a turbulent recovery, with shingles and all.'

'I am still really tired, Nanna, from the low iron levels, but I am getting there. I have lost all the hair on my arms and legs from this DH. I am still doing my TAFE diesel fitter course and working part-time here in town. Everything is improving, but to keep my immune system high and further attacks of the shingles away, the doctor said, "No stress".'

Pop said encouragingly, 'Lizzy said you had put on about eight kilograms. I couldn't imagine you being thinner.'

'Yes, to be 185 cm tall and weigh only 55 kg was a shock. I was naturally expecting to get better after my appendix came out. Then every time I ate, my gut ached, I got bloated or had diarrhoea. With what the doctor called malabsorption, I became foggy headed. I could never have sorted this diet out by myself. I couldn't even think straight. I had the worst memory. I was forever looking to find stuff; it was maddening. At my worst, the tiles seemed to be moving on the floor. I got a bit dizzy, so I couldn't even drive. I have been very dependent on Chloe.'

'Well, we are all glad you are getting better. We really appreciate all that Chloe has done for you. You're right, there is no reason to rush into anything.'

'I'm glad Chloe found a beer we can all have together,' Pop interjected. 'It tastes pretty good, doesn't it?'

Lionel and Keith nodded and smiled in agreement.

After such a lovely day, Keith was surprised when Chloe suddenly left the table at dinner. He found her in his bedroom in tears.

'Are you all right, honey?' Keith said compassionately, looking concerned.

'Yes, yes,' said Chloe, tearful but smiling. 'I am being

stupid,' she said, wiping her sodden face. 'I have really enjoyed today. I am overwhelmed by all the beautiful gifts, the lovely people, the fun and cheerful joking ... real family stuff that I haven't had for years.'

'Yes, they are an amazing bunch,' Keith confirmed, hugging her.

'They are all so ... so ... welcoming and affectionate. It's like the Christmas days we had when Dad was alive,' she sobbed.

'They all love you for who you are, Chloe, not because I'm your partner. They noticed that you bought gluten-free Christmas pudding and Christmas cake, and the gluten-free beers that none of us knew existed, so I could have a drink with my family and not feel like an alien. They were such clever gifts.'

'Yes, it has been a lovely day.'

'Mmm ... while I don't want to leave you, I know they will be worrying. I'll just tell them you are going to ring your family, shall I?'

'Yes. Thank you for understanding. Tell them that nothing is wrong'.

'Is Chloe okay?' Lizzy asked.

'Nothing is wrong, Mum, Chloe just misses her parents more at holiday times. She said she is glad I grew up with such an incredible family.' Keith looked around. 'I do feel very blessed.'

Lizzy gave Keith a warm hug.

'Chloe's just going to ring her brothers and sister to catch up with them now,' Keith said, kissing his mother's cheek. 'It has been the best day, Mum. This has been the best ending to this roller-coaster year.'

Chapter 30

Chloe

C hloe's psychological growth continued with her next evening shift. She was developing a greater awareness of how many traumatised and dysfunctional people existed in the world. A young twenty-one-year-old woman was admitted, wheeled in on a stretcher, loudly recalling all her drug overdose attempts, she had initiated to gain the attention she craved. One of the pregnant nurses, Julie, was allocated to look after the young patient with challenging behaviours, since she would only require continuous cardiac monitoring in the ICU, not lifting.

'Get me a drink, slut,' the patient ordered. Ignoring her behaviour, Julie got her a drink. The young woman, keen to attract further unwarranted attention, continued insulting the staff. Kathy, an ICU nurse with extensive experience in caring for psychiatric patients, walked past, hearing the disrespect.

'What are you looking at you, moron?' the disrespectful patient queried.

'Hey, I'm paid to be here! Who's the moron?' Kathy instantly fired back.

Involuntary giggles erupted in the nearby bedside spaces, with other critically ill patients entertained at the quick-witted response.

'I wish I had your quick comebacks,' said Chloe.

'It's intolerance,' Kathy replied, hoping the patient could hear. 'No one will ever pay me enough to tolerate eight hours of that rot, even though she has a behavioural problem, a personality disorder.'

'You are good for us, Kathy. You teach us all how we should be treated,' Chloe said. 'It's funny that no one ever teaches us that. You'd think we should know it instinctively.'

'I am not making light of her suicide attempts. However, we are all worthy of being treated with respect. I accept nothing less,' replied Kathy, slinging her arm over Chloe's shoulders in a comradely gesture. 'You teach people how you want to be treated. There were more than five people ready to take down that mad cow the other day, because you are an absolute asset. We all appreciate the hard work you put in Chloe, especially the way you support the juniors. Sometimes, we don't tell people how much we appreciate them. I, for one, am determined to be better!'

'Thank you. You are so kind.'

'You are so worth it. Now, Chloe!' Kathy said, changing subjects, 'I am jumping out of my skin to ask – who was that tall, totally drop-dead gorgeous guy I saw you with downstairs on Thursday at the canteen?'

'My partner, Keith.'

'Well done, you!' Kathy nudged Chloe with her elbow, achieving a shy smile. 'Is he as nice as he looks? More importantly, does he have a brother?'

'Yes, he is, and his younger brother your age is already taken, unfortunately.'

'Shame. Keith looks like a keeper.'

'He definitely is. I've never felt so loved and appreciated. Keith and his whole family have been very welcoming. It has been such a novel experience to be accepted for who I am.'

'And that is how you deserve to be treated, each and every day. No exceptions.'

Chapter 31

Chloe and Keith

U nanimously, the Johnson family had insisted on putting in fifty dollars each to contribute to a jewellery gift for Chloe, leaving Keith to pay for only the ring when she chose it. While all the Johnsons had secretly thought the pearl earrings and bracelet would make excellent wedding day jewellery, the decision was up to the enchanting couple.

Chloe had loved both Sheila and Keith's choices, since sapphires were her birthstone. Sheila had left her family's contributions at the jewellers, surprising both Keith and Chloe when they visited on 27 December. No one wanted to hasten a marriage or entrap either Keith or Chloe into a lifelong commitment, even though it seemed inevitable.

Once again, Chloe was overwhelmed at the generosity and beauty of the Johnson family. Tears filled her eyes and her right hand covered her mouth as she forced herself to swallow. Chloe had to take a deep breath through pursed lips. Their kindness had rekindled in the orphan the loving memories she had been blessed with from both her natural parents. The emotion generated by their generosity triggered a mixture of beauty and grief. Chloe was often amazed by how she experienced such conflicting emotions like love and fear together.

The two sets of earrings, one Ceylon sapphire and one pearl were purchased, along with the Ceylon sapphire ring and an elegant matching pearl bracelet. After they left the jewellers, with all items still in their boxes, Chloe and Keith decided to dine at the mall coffee shop for breakfast.

'That was an overwhelming surprise, wasn't it?' Chloe shared with Keith.

'Yes, delightful and unexpected. Do you want to go to Mum and Dad's tomorrow to thank everyone?'

'Yes, absolutely. Your family is so lovely and welcoming, so supportive of each other.'

'Yes, they are. So, my darling on which finger are you going to put this heart-shaped Ceylon sapphire?' Keith looked intensely into Chloe's eyes, maintaining her gaze. 'I do want to marry you. I love you. I also want you to have all the time you need to make that decision. This is not a pressure for commitment question. This is an "I love you, what do you want to do" question. I feel so incomplete without you. I don't mean that in a dependent way. I am simply saying that it is so pleasurable to love you and be with you every day. I do want to live the rest of my life with you, to make a beautiful home with you and marry you Chloe Barnett.'

Chloe opened the box and passed it back to Keith, holding out both hands with her fingers splayed. 'I have chosen the pace of all the other parts of our relationship. This is a big decision, one that you get to choose.'

When Keith slipped the beautiful eighteen-karat ring on Chloe's left hand as an engagement ring, a tear of joy spilled down her cheek. Whereas Chloe had always feared rejection, Keith held both her hands, with his charismatic smile spreading to the corners of his eyes.

'As my dad used to tell me, "I love you to the moon and back", Keith.'

'You make me truly happy,' he replied, pressing his soft lips on hers lightly.

Cozied up in the lounge chairs of the coffee shop, Keith planted a more longing kiss on Chloe's lips.

'Let's just spend this day together to celebrate.'

'It is truly an amazing feeling to feel wanted,' Chloe admitted. 'Irate Irene made us feel worthless and devalued most of our lives. This feels like the other extreme.'

'What I was always told about dealing with destructive people like that, Chloe, is to be glad you don't live inside their head.'

'I like that thought. It recognises that Irene always possessed an unhealthy mindset. As a child always getting hurt and supposedly "disciplined", you believe that you are the problem, not the criminal adult. Do you know, the other day when she called me her niece, I realised with shock that I have never, ever, even thought of her in any role. Not as an aunty, not as a mother, not even as a relative. I don't believe any of us did. She was just always Irate Irene. As children, we all just considered her a vile monster, like the ones we saw in the cartoons at Dad's.'

'The only valuable thing Irene taught you all was resilience and to protect yourselves. You all took back your power when you removed yourselves from her disturbing behaviours.'

'I guess I will always feel guilty about being the first to relocate.'

'I think your appearance of looking like your mother probably made you the most at risk. As a child, you were also instinctively protecting yourself from the monster.'

'Yes, I lived in fear. Irene was nasty, vicious and manipulating.'

'And you should never feel guilty for removing yourself from an unsafe situation.'

'Did you ever want children?' Chloe asked.

'Not really. Don't get me wrong; I have the most amazing family. We will both have plenty of nephews and nieces to love and care for. One of my thoughts after I was diagnosed was that I don't think I would really want a child, to have to grow up worrying about every bite of food they ate, like I now have to. If you ever change your mind and decide you wanted to have children, I would support you and love them. Our future can be anything we want. However, whether we have or don't have children is not a deal breaker for me after I inherited dad's dodgy genes.'

'I am glad you feel that way. I see children as defenceless pawns in adult power games. I survived a childhood that I would never wish on anyone!'

'When we tell my parents we are engaged, what do you want to do if they want to have an engagement party? My parents have a "celebrate life while you're here" mentality.'

'Oh, I don't know. Neither of us are party people, really.'

'We could all go out for a large family dinner on St Valentine's Day. That would be romantic.'

'That's a good idea ... or a barbecue.'

'Yes, something quiet with no crowds and no work for anyone. It would be good just to enjoy each other's company by going out for a meal. That way your mum and dad won't be doing a lot of cooking and cleaning before or afterwards.'

'Nanna will ask about when we want to get married. She will be really excited,' laughed Keith. 'What do you want to do? We can have a long engagement or just leave the wedding date open.'

'Open sounds good. It would be good to save up and put a deposit on a home first. I don't need a big elaborate wedding. After our father died, I have badly wanted a place to call home. We will tell everyone that we are just taking one step at a time.'

'I'm very excited. My future is looking better every day since I met you.'

'I used to struggle through every day, trying to avoid people. Now I dream about having a three-bedroom brick house with a double garage,' laughed Chloe.

'And a big three-bay shed?'

'Sounds good!'

'Two dogs,' smiled Keith.

'Absolutely!'

'We could photograph your hand and press "send",' teased Keith.

'That will light up our phones!'

'They will ring all day! Everyone will be so excited. That way, we could tell both families at the same time on our own phones. I reckon I only need to do three texts for the news to travel fast – Nanna, Sheila and Mum!'

'Okay,' said Chloe, holding out her hand. Keith sent the images. Nanna and Pop surprised them both by being the first callers to congratulate the happy couple. Nanna was excitedly asking so many questions that it was difficult to keep track.

'Thank you, Nanna, Pop,' both responded. 'No, it's only just happened.'

'I am so excited. We both are. You both make such a cute couple. I was hoping on Boxing Day when we saw you both together that this would be permanent.'

Keith and Chloe listened to their cheerful conversations between themselves, hearing Pop ask if any dates for an engagement party had been set.

'We are thinking about going out for a meal together on St Valentine's Day, Pop, so that no one is cooking or working. We will just have to see if Sheila can get that evening off first.'

'How romantic!' Nanna adds, approving of our choice.

'It doesn't need to be a restaurant. Any pub with gluten-free meals would be fine,' Chloe suggested. 'Keith and I both like quiet occasions rather than big parties.'

'We should mention that house hunting will probably be our next priority,' Keith said. 'We can both access salary sacrifice arrangements with our employers. That means the mortgage gets paid out of our wages before tax is taken out.'

'Oh, that sounds good, dear. It's all very exciting.'

Beeping on Keith's phone alerted him that Lizzy and Lionel were trying to get through.

'Congratulations and yahoooooo!' Keith's parents shouted together.

Chloe suddenly had a sickening feeling in her gut.

'Oh God!' Chloe said, looking alarmed. 'We should have told Sheila in person. After what happened when Brett died, she may feel alone and sad.'

'Oh, I should have thought of that too!' gasped Keith. 'I am kicking myself now.'

'Sheila wanted you two to be together,' Lionel and Lizzy reassured them. 'She has had a devastating loss, but Sheila would never want you both to put your lives on hold because she is heartbroken.'

'It was probably silly sending her a picture like that. It could upset her. We might go back to the unit and check.'

'Is Sheila working? She may not have got the message yet. Trust me, she will be enthralled, not upset,' Lizzy insisted over the phone. 'Sheila has wanted to see your relationship blossom for months. This terrific news will be like her dream come true.'

'I didn't check when she was working, Mum. We would not want to hurt Sheila for the world!'

'That's another reason for low key celebrations. Poor Sheila's engagement celebrations were almost a pivotal moment in Brett's tragedy. You know, this morning we were talking about putting a deposit on a house. We have been talking about a three-bedroom brick house, or we could get a house with a granny flat that Sheila could move into. That would be better than her living alone. Let's see if Sheila is interested.'

'What about Gabby?' Keith asked.

'Her boyfriend, Josh, has already been asking to move into our unit.'

Chloe and Keith dash back to find Sheila outside washing her car with earbuds in, listening to music.

Relieved and grinning, they approach her. Seeing them both smiling, Sheila looks automatically for the ring.

'Brilliant!' Sheila raced over to hug them both.

'Oh my God! This is epic,' said Sheila, as they helped Sheila rinse her car before going inside to make plans. Sheila was keen on the granny flat idea to give the new lovers privacy.

'A granny flat would let me move out of these nursing units and rest more after the night shifts. It would be low maintenance, and we can ask Mum and Dad about bringing our pets to stay.'

Jake was also delighted to hear his little sister had become engaged. Using his accounting skills, Jake crunched the numbers for a home loan on his calculator

'Your combined income would be too large to get a first home buyer's assistance package,' Jake said. 'You will need to add legal fees, do property pest inspections and check for flood zones and property debts on rates and utilities. With you both able to salary sacrifice, and if we estimate Sheila contributing $150 a week, a mortgage of $400,000 would allow you to pay no more than the standard third of your income each fortnight.'

As an engagement gift, Jake mapped out a saving plan that allowed Chloe and Keith to manage their finances while paying a reducing balance that would allow them to eventually own their home. After congratulatory wishes were shared, Vera and Georgie expressed their wish to share the cost of engagement photos for the new couple.

Keith's family understood Chloe's need to prioritise a home. Three months later, they found their ideal three-bedroom brick home with an attached granny flat. The property featured a large backyard with plenty of space to build the three-bay shed that Keith desired, using their next tax return. With the council rates, building and pest inspections performed, the legal fees were paid and the thirty-day cooling off interval began. Chloe moved into Keith's room, allowing Josh to move into hers, so that more income could be saved for utility bonds.

Before they could move into their new house, Sheila collected the keys. When Chloe and Keith entered, they found that Sheila and Gordie had mischievously placed a framed photo of Keith with the sleeping Chloe in her satin nightie on the dressing table. On the wall above the bed, they had mounted one of Jill's professionally framed pictures of Chloe in the white satin night dress with her legs draped over a gigantic teddy bear, whose right arm was propped on her shoulder.

'Do they think I need help with my libido?' asked Keith, amused at their antics. He moved in to give Chloe another opportunistic hug. 'Are we moving the puppies in too?'

'If your mum and dad won't mind? They can hang out together while we are at work. With this property situated in a cul-de-sac, there won't be a lot of people and traffic going past for them to bark at.'

'Let's check with Sheila. We could bring them over last, so there will be less risk of them getting distressed from the strange environment while we are coming and going.'

The puppies moved in, sleeping in the granny flat with Sheila at night when she was home. In Chloe and Keith's master bedroom, the presence of a bookcase ledge between the wall and their bed left a space where the puppies liked to go for a quiet sleep. Until their hiding spot was found, it seemed like Rosie and Julian appeared from nowhere to greet them all as they got home from work. There was a small hole built in the garage wall where two bricks were missing that the previous owners had designed to allow their own pets to toilet. Since there were no pet friendly gaps in the granny flat walls, Rosie and Julian had to wait at the door for Sheila to open it, to enter and exit. The puppy were to be collected last, to prevent Vera, Georgie, Gordie and Jake tripping over the exuberant canines.

On November 26th, Vera and Georgie returned to Gympie for a planned dinner with partners to remember the anniversary of their father's death. Vera stayed at Jake's house and Georgie bunked down in Chloe and Keith's spare bedroom. For Georgie, Jake and Vera, helping to shift Keith and Chloe had provided a welcome reprieve from the sadness of their first get-together since their father's death. Losing their father, their family home and Vera's sudden separation from Danny had left all siblings in survival mode after John's death. While Chloe, Sheila and Keith packed up their belongings in boxes for the move, Vera, Georgie, Jake and Keith's younger brother, Gordie, transported all the items in two vehicles. Chloe, Sheila and Keith also gave her unit a final clean, before the new tenants arrived the following day.

With many hands on deck, making the transition smooth and fast, they decided to end the busy day with Keith and Chloe meeting them for hot drinks at 4 pm at the corner store before the Barnett evening remembrance meal. Sheila and Gordie returned the unit keys to the real estate agent, so that Keith and Chloe could order the warm drinks and pay. While Vera and Keith had gone into the combined grocery and coffee shop, Chloe, Jake and Georgie had waited outside at the picnic tables to keep some bench seats available for Gordie and Sheila's return.

It was only while Chloe was watching her sister climbing the store front stairs that she saw the familiar small blue sedan arrive. As Willie Chambers exited his vehicle, Chloe realised he had seen Vera entering the store. Launching onto her feet, Chloe raced over the car park into the mini supermarket, searching for her sister. Georgie and Jake, alerted by Chloe's alarmed expression and instant flight, followed suit. Willie was stealthily moving closer to Vera who had her back to him, removing milk from the dairy fridge. He was intending to catch her off guard. As Willie furtively snuck forward to advance towards Vera, the three tall shadows of Jake, Keith and Georgie blocked the ceiling light as they loomed over him.

'Come out to the parking lot, sunshine,' Keith invited in a menacing tone, distracting Willie's focus on Vera.

Willie looked up to find himself surrounded with no place to go.

'I was just shopping,' said Willie, attempting to feign innocence.

'Cruising for a bruising, all right! And I'm more than happy to oblige you,' the bulky, muscled Georgie replied, as he placed both hands on his hips, expanding his buffed biceps to the size of Willie's thighs.

'I saw him first.'

Jake advanced with a condescending steely gaze, looking keenly down on the wiry Willie.

'You're out of chances, Willie,' Vera warned. 'You'll feel sorry for roadkill if you try this again.'

'You lot can't threaten me!' Willie shouted, playing the victim.

'No threats here, just free body sculpting for misogynists,' Jake added in a menacing tone.

'You'll keep,' threatened Willie.

'Oh, no need to wait, sunshine! Come out to the parking lot now. I can get you dusted off in about ten seconds,' Georgie volunteered sarcastically through clenched teeth.

The cowardly Willie made a hasty retreat, leaving the shop without any purchases.

Chapter 32

Chloe and Willie

Chloe was especially contented to finally have what she had always longed for, a place to call home. Sharing this dream home with Keith, Sheila and the puppies made her happier than she had ever thought possible. Life was blissful. Every afternoon or morning, depending on the shifts she was working, Chloe grew accustomed to being welcomed home by the puppies, with balls or stuffed toys in their gobs, keen to get a game going.

It was therefore odd, a month later, when Chloe arrived home with Sheila after their eight-hour day shift to find no frantic tails wagging in greeting. The silence was deafening. Sheila had gone straight into her granny flat for a shower, before the girls would be getting together to organise the evening meal, ready for when Keith arrived home. Feeling something was amiss, Chloe felt the hair prickle up on the back of her neck. Reaching for the intercom between the house and the granny flat, Chloe attempted to alert Sheila that something was wrong.

As Chloe picked up the phone, a force slammed into her, knocking her onto the king-size bed in their main bedroom. As Chloe began to turn over, a fist punched her left cheek, leaving her shocked. Next, Willie Chambers launched himself onto her body, pinning her wrists down with his knees. He leaned forward – just as Chloe struck his nose with her head. When he backed off out of reach, holding his bloodied face, Chloe delivered a head-high kick with her legs, slamming Willie backwards into the wardrobe behind him. Chloe rolled off the other side of the bed, away from him.

Feeling confident with Chloe still on the ground, Willie moved forward, not knowing that Chloe's monthly self-defence classes had taught her never to try to get up, if on the ground. Using her legs, Chloe slammed another kick, forcing his left knee backwards in an abnormal direction. Willie howled, swore and exploded in a vicious temper.

'Call the police,' Chloe shouted, hoping Sheila would hear her through the intercom. 'It's Willie Chambers.'

Willie began violently hurling perfume bottles, moisturisers and heavier items off the dressing table. When he turned to pick up another missile, Chloe attacked his left knee again, buckling it to bring him down. Thankfully, Willie managed to fall away from the door. Chloe exited rapidly, grabbing her bag on the way through the lounge, heading outside to use her mobile phone. Sheila met her at the door, causing Chloe to trip when the door opened before she could reach the handle. They collided.

'Use your phone. Get the police,' Chloe shouted. When they raced towards the neighbours, they discovered Willie had parked his car in front of their place. Seeing no weapons around, Chloe removed a garden paver to hurl, just as Willie appeared limping in the doorway. With the sound of distant police sirens now becoming faintly audible, Willy headed towards his car limping at a painful pace. Feeling less threatened than she had in the confined bedroom, Chloe placed the thick paver in front of the front passenger wheel. Willie continued his advance, swearing profusely and delivering vile threats. Unperturbed, Chloe chocked a second garden paver under the driver's front wheel, to ensure Willie remained at their house until the police arrived. When Willie reached his car, Sheila threw another paver at the windscreen, shattering the glass to stop Willie from driving away. Willie changed direction, advancing on Chloe, who was the closest after placing another thick paver in front of the back passenger wheel.

Seeing two women under attack, an elderly male neighbour came out swinging his five-iron golf club, delivering a strong blow to Willie's turned back. Willie shrieked, attracting more attention from the other cul de sac residents. A young male resident from the other side of the cul-de-sac appeared, on the phone talking to the police. When she heard them describing the offender as a middle-aged male, 160 cm tall, dark olive complexion with black jeans and a navy shirt, Chloe called out, 'William Chambers, it's William Chambers. He has a long history of assaults and domestic violence.' The strong, buffed neighbour promptly finished his call and tackled Willie to the ground. When the police arrived, Willie was pinned down and yelling in pain. The ambulance arrived soon afterwards to transport Willie to the hospital to receive medical attention for his knee injury.

Chloe was uncertain how Willie had gained entry to their home until the police discovered the guest window had been smashed with a pot plant. The glass and the pot plant had both been concealed behind the floor length curtains. Chloe dashed into the bedroom, looking behind the bed to find that Julian was moving fretfully. Rosie was shaking and softly whimpering. The police helped Chloe and Sheila push the king-side bed back to pick up Rosie. Rosie yelped and began quivering violently.

A neighbour's surveillance camera showed Willie arriving at 2.45 pm. Julian had barked continuously but remained out of reach.

As Rosie approached barking, Willie had viciously kicked her in the ribs after he had entered their side gate. The vet found Willie had fractured five of Rosie's ribs. Poor little Rosie took a good six weeks to recover. Rosie and Julian went back to Lionel and Lizzy's home until Sheila, Chloe or Keith had days off to make sure someone was available to maintain her pain relief.

Willie's image recorded on camera footage throwing the pot plant through the guest room window was also retrieved as evidence to be used in court. After Sheila provided a statement testifying that they had arrived home from work together, the police photographed Chloe's bruised cheek, face and arm contusions. These injuries were inflicted as she shielded herself against the missiles Willie had pelted at her. Chloe's cousin, Margaret from CIB, who had collated multiple statements from the Barnett and Johnson families following Willie's previous attempts at intimidation, was determined that this time he would be stopped.

Sheila and Chloe had just returned from the hospital, where Chloe's facial injuries had been X-rayed, as Keith drove into the garage. He had been instantly shocked at the site of Chloe's facial and arm contusions. Keith was furious. He intended to speak to the police himself to make sure that Willie was stopped. Keeping Sheila and Chloe with him, Keith drove over to his parents to get a large sheet of ply board to seal the broken window space. Chloe was not so much shaken as livid that Willie had invaded her personal space. She had had a gutful of him being continually permitted by the courts to be free to stalk her and her sister. Keith was relieved to notice that Chloe appeared to be buzzing more from toxic adrenaline levels than fear.

After his knee restoration surgery, Willie was charged the following day, at a hospital bedside hearing where he remained under police guard, with trespassing onto private property, breaking and entering, assault, grievous bodily harm and animal cruelty. After his court hearing, Willie found himself sentenced to jail without parole for ten years as a repeat offender. Willie's sister, Karen, assumed the custodianship for his children, who tragically had always seemed to be Willy's least priority.

In court, the police psychologist, examining his record of re-offending, described Willie Chambers as having an antisocial personality disorder. The psychologist explained that criminals with antisocial personality disorders like Willie were difficult to sway, since they show no concern for others. Besides lacking empathy, another dominant trait was that they were unwilling to learn from their mistakes. Since anti-social personality disorders lacked insight into their offensive behaviours, they often cycled through prisons and counselling, with neither punishment nor reflection making an iota of difference. She explained that criminals with antisocial personality disorders demonstrated a remarkable ability to keep repeating their offences without learning from them, because they didn't consider their lying, stealing or aggression to be wrong.

Following the assault, Keith, Chloe and Sheila attended kick boxing and self-defence classes monthly. Keith was in no doubt that Chloe felt triumphant and successful. Since no one could change Willie's anti-social personality disorder, they needed to feel confident in learning to protect themselves.

That was why the only social interaction Chloe had, prior to meeting Keith, was to go to self-defence classes fortnightly. Since she could not change Willie's stalking behaviours, she was determined to become more confident in learning to protect herself.

Chapter 33

Chloe

C hloe intuitively felt that she had come full circle. Her family network was becoming as extensive as her friendships with nursing colleagues. Social isolation was no longer a necessary shield. Chloe welcomed Keith's touch, whether he was rubbing his hands along her back, pressing his soft lips against hers or simply holding her hands. The intimate contact was subtle and gentle, and missed when he was not there. Chloe noticed daily how the presence of Keith and his family made her life complete. From the first day of meeting Keith's parents, unless Chloe was on night shifts, the couple cuddled and spent almost every moment together. Chloe was unable to regress to her trademark detached self with so many caring people in her company.

The warm Johnson family had welcomed the Barnett

family, offering accommodation and inclusion in the planning of the wedding arrangements.

On the wedding morning, Chloe, Vera as matron of honour, and Gabby and Sheila as bridesmaids dressed at Nanna and Pop's house. Lizzy, Nanna, the bride, the matron of honour and the bridesmaids all had their nails varnished, hair set and make-up applied together. In a show of unity, they chose the same subtle, plum pink colour for their nails and matching lipsticks. Along with Jill they all chose Chloe's lingerie from a specialty lingerie shop. Chloe did not get to see these items until her wedding day when, with the courage of two glasses of champagne, there could be no refusal of the strapless sweetheart bust on the lace-up corset.

The girls conspired to video and record phone photos for Keith as Chloe opened their bridal gift, gasping at the sexy white satin and lace negligee they had all chosen. As Nanna chortled, Chloe went beetroot-red, rapidly gulping down the last remnants of her second champagne. The white satin nightie featured narrow shoulder straps, a plunging cleavage and white, see-through lace up both sides, which continued from the hem to the armholes. The effect was erotic and daring.

'Good lord, Keith's going to have a coronary,' gasped Chloe as a red blotchy rash climbed her neck.

She sat there, shyly appreciating the beautiful sexy garment they had all agreed on. Everyone burst out laughing when bashful Chloe looked in the box for matching knickers that did not exist! Nanna, who had strategically removed them from the box before it was gift-wrapped, was especially amused.

'You weren't looking for knickers?' Nanna asked, deadpan.

Nanna jovially pulled the sheer lace briefs that matched the sheer side lace of the negligee out of her handbag. The girls cheered loudly and hooted excitedly as the mottled rash climbed further up Chloe's neck.

'You had me squirming, Nanna, you demon!' laughed Chloe, giving her a hug.

Nanna, Sheila and Lizzy had found Chloe the most beautiful wedding dress. Having worn white as a student nurse, and checking Chloe's skin tones, the ladies all decided that an almond-coloured satin dress would be more elegant. The dress had lace from the sweetheart neckline to the neck, at the hem of the dress and on the abundant skirt, dyed in coffee to make the lace visible on the wedding photos. The shiny gathered leg-of-mutton sleeves and the matching tiara headpiece added to the stunning dress. The pink, mauve and white floral baskets carried by the bride and bridesmaids were displayed throughout the Salvation Army citadel, on the marriage certificate signing table and beside the gluten-free wedding cake.

Keith, Jake and Georgie looked handsome and refined in their almond-coloured shirts and jackets with aquamarine bowties, champagne-coloured roses and black trousers. The men's aquamarine pocket decorations and belts blended with Sheila and Vera's dresses.

Nanna had placed an ivory-beaded, horseshoe-shaped

charm on Chloe's arm with a ribbon for her traditional 'something old item' to symbolise good luck. Chloe wore the pearl earrings and bracelet as her 'something new' item to signify her bonding with the Johnson family, who had all contributed to the purchase of that gorgeous gift. The 'something borrowed' item was Vera's ivory-coloured netted veil attached to the tiara, while the 'something blue' item was the garter with a blue ribbon worn on Chloe's thigh. The bride's wedding band was specially made by a jeweller to navigate the heart-shaped Ceylon sapphire engagement ring.

Vera had also brought a bride doll dressed in a wedding dress with a veil that went over the doll's face before the wedding and was pulled back after the wedding. The bridal doll was displayed in the back windscreen of the bridal car. Two posh bride and groom teddy bears were anchored with white ribbons to the bonnets of the bride's and groom's antique 1946 Ford Deluxe cars owned by Pop.

Nanna got her Mills and Boon fix, watching Chloe walk down the citadel aisle to Kenny Rogers singing about her knight in shining armour who loved her. Nanna sang along as Pop looked on tenderly.

The groom's meal on their wedding day was gluten-free and delicious. The bride and groom's wedding table was arranged in a horseshoe pattern, with the Johnson and Barnett families seated on each side of the bride and groom. Chloe was pleased to see Keith's family tentatively approaching and introducing themselves to Chloe's siblings and their families.

Other tables inside the horseshoe were dedicated for

nurses and friends. A photo of the male and female bridal teddy bears was replicated on the place and table settings. Intrigued by their choice in table cards, Lizzy and Lionel picked theirs up to find personal, handwritten messages from Chloe on the back. Lizzy's message read, 'You make beautiful babies, xx'; Lionel's read, 'Another son stolen, xx.' Keith had written on Nanny's, 'I am wondering what mischief you will get up to' followed by an emoji smiley face, with kisses from Chloe as well. Sheila's said, 'Thank you for my white satin lady, xx, Keith.'

On the wedding invitations, Keith and Chloe had specified that, instead of gifts, donations for the Salvation Army were preferred to assist those struggling financially, like single mothers, low income groups and the homeless. The wedding table was therefore stacked high with nappies, singlets, sleeping bags, blankets, toiletries, puffer jackets, raincoats and umbrellas for the homeless. Lizzy and Lionel keenly cuddled the smaller children to assist with family photos at the ceremony. When Jill approached Chloe, asking for a picture of Chloe with Georgie's infant, Chloe instantly recognised that something seemed amiss. Why wouldn't Jill be inviting Keith to be in the photo also? With Chloe's back to the bridal party, Sheila snuck around to give Keith the large, wrapped present she had kept hidden inside her vehicle. That gift was not to go onto the table with the wedding presents. After the picture was taken, the suspicious Chloe turned around, surprised to see Keith unwrapping a large gift presented to him by Sheila. Nanny, Pop, Lizzy and

Lionel had their heads laid back chortling. Keith's expression was of one smitten. He looked at Chloe, his face glowing with a sexy smile. Recognising that another prank had been played, Chloe dashed up to see what had everyone's attention, conscious that Jill was still flashing her camera. Partially concealed in Keith's lap was an enlarged photo of Chloe in her grass bra, skirt and thongs, lined with the small pink fabric flowers. Keith was delighted. He had always wanted that picture. The gang had obviously saved the best for last.

When they arrived back from their honeymoon, that picture was mounted next to the white satin lady picture above their bed. In between the two Chloe photos was a picture of a tanned, shirtless Keith on the Cairns esplanade on their honeymoon. Keith was wearing sunglasses, board shorts and a beach towel draped over his tanned shoulders. While the photos were initially instigated to elevate Chloe's self-esteem, Keith's body image also benefited after his dramatic weight loss.

Conclusion

On her wedding day, Chloe had looked around at Vera, Jake and Georgie seated with their families. She observed that none of their children were being strictly disciplined. As the evening drew on, exhausted toddlers fell asleep in loving arms. Each toddler approached their parents, lifting their arms, visually displaying how much they felt cherished. While younger children played together or clung to cuddly toys, older children were distracted using their electronic devices. Irate Irene's legacy of child abuse had not been recycled onto further generations. All the children were well groomed and dressed in the family wedding photos, which Chloe and Keith had got enlarged and framed as presents.

While Vera, Jake and Georgie had been psychologically traumatised by hostile Irene, none had resorted to cigarette smoking, alcohol or the use of illicit drugs as a coping mechanism. Chloe was immensely proud that each of her siblings was living productive lives. Not only were they all exemplary role models for their children, but as nurturing parents, all had encouraged their offspring to develop community-minded behaviours.

Unfortunately, Ross had two further heart attacks within five years of his original intensive care admission. Ross's quality of life continually declined as the cardiac failure caused breathlessness, reducing his ability to mobilise. Ross and Irene ended up living in independent care in a nursing home village complex. As their level of care needed to be escalated due to the aging process and Ross's heart attacks, they were both transferred to the higher dependency areas.

After Ross died, few visitors were willing to ruin their day listening to Irate Irene's self-righteous verbal dialogue. Even the caregivers, who normally encouraged the elderly to mobilise and socialise in the main dining room, tended to leave Irene set up to dine in her room alone. The need to isolate the inflammatory Irene for her own protection became apparent after one of her evening tirades. One of the quieter elderly gentlemen, who had never raised a holler, became intolerant of her rants. The thin elderly male returned from the kitchen and had pitched five eggs at Irene before he could be stopped. Irene had stopped in the middle of her tirade, shocked, looking down at the egg albumen and yolks dripping off her frock. Taken by surprise, Irene had looked up at the man, stunned, only to see more hurling towards her as the other residents became inspired by his example.

Not realising what was happening, the nurses were already

occupied and unable to leave the elderly patients they were mobilising back to their rooms. Therefore, the bombardment continued. Several other nursing home residents wandered to the egg carton, intending to launch a few missiles themselves.

'What are you doing, Henry?' asked a nurse, frustrated that she could not leave a dependent resident without risking a fall.

'If you won't stop this absurd nag, we will,' Henry replied unapologetically.

'Cut that out, Bertie,' cried another nurse, twisting to find the nearest chair for her patient, as she observed him pitching another raw egg.

'Martha,' pleaded another nurse, 'you know better than that!'

'I know better than to miss, Sally! This could be my one shot at this obnoxious hypocrite!'

Irene just stood there, dazed, as eggs rained down upon her, shattering eggshells and contents to the floor.

From the age of ninety years, Irene's fellow inpatients felt blessed when a minor stroke rendered her non-verbal. Since the devil was in no hurry to take his own back, the demented Irene existed to the ripe old age of ninety-seven years, when, ironically, a metastatic breast cancer spread to her brain. It was only when Irene had lost consciousness that her children and grandchildren arrived to pay her a final visit. All Irene's children and grandchildren avoided the term 'final respects', because they had none.

Not one of the Barnett family members acknowledged any

kinship to Irate Irene. When she died, Vera, Jake, Chloe and Georgie were just glad to have the infestation of the abusive Irene out of their lives. It was almost as though their physical and psychological wounds could finally now heal.

Many factors had contributed to Irene's brutality and weaponising of religion. After Irene's father had been unable to obtain work, feeling like a failure, he had simply abandoned his wife and five daughters to starve. For the rest of her life, Irene had raged against those feelings of rejection and having to chronically exist with her choices constrained by poverty. Being one of so many children of the same gender, Irene had weaponised her lack of education, her loud foghorn voice and society's devotion to religion to demand the attention she had felt deprived of.

Since Irene had spent her whole life expecting to be rejected, she had unwittingly compensated by developing behaviours to facilitate that outcome. When her craving attention, using bad behaviours was rewarded, she generated more. Ross, who had protected Bella when his older brother Len ignored her, was perpetually used to rescuing maidens in distress. He failed to challenge Irene's malicious conduct, making him her ideal partner. In this pathological relationship, both had their needs met. Irene was therefore excessively jealous of the educated, talented Bella who was very loved by Ross and her parents.

Since 1991, social security entitlements have been extended by successive governments to include provisions for single parents, job seekers, veterans and the disabled. The *Child*

Protection Act 1999 introduced the mandatory reporting of child abuse by professionals into legislation. Although this act, to protect the safety of children and young people from harm or the risk of harm from individuals not willing or able to protect them, was too late for the Barnett family, too many children's lives and quality of life still remain in danger. Child safety officers receiving complaints now have an official duty of care to investigate and report any incidences of alleged child abuse and neglect. Reporting children at risk is both a professional and community responsibility.